Alice in Time

Alice in Time

by Penelope Bush

Holiday House / New York

ALICE IN TIME by Penelope Bush was first published in the United Kingdom
in 2010. This North American edition is published by arrangement with
Piccadilly Press Limited, London, England.

Text copyright © Penelope Bush, 2010
First published in the United States by Holiday House, Inc. in 2011.
All Rights Reserved
HOLIDAY HOUSE is registered in the U.S. Patent and Trademark Office.
The text typeface is Stempel Schneidler.
Printed and bound in December 2010 at Maple Vail, York, PA, USA.
www.holidayhouse.com
First American Edition
1   3   5   7   9   10   8   6   4   2

Library of Congress Cataloging-in-Publication Data
Bush, Penelope.
Alice in time / by Penelope Bush.—1st American ed.
p. cm.
Summary: As her self-centered behavior spirals out of control, fourteen-year-old
Alice gets an unusal chance to fix her whole disastrous life when she is mysteriously
spirited back in time.
ISBN 978-0-8234-2329-3 (hardcover)
[1. Conduct of life—Fiction.   2. Self-perception—Fiction.   3. Single-parent
families—Fiction.   4. Interpersonal relations—Fiction.   5. Time travel—
Fiction.   6. England—Fiction.]   I. Title.
PZ7.B96544A1 2011
[Fic]—dc22
2010023666

For Helen Percival, a wonderful
English teacher, whose belief
in me has had a lasting effect

Alice in Time

PART 1

Chapter One

"I'm *not* wearing it."

"Yes, you are."

"No, I'm not."

Repeat those last two sentences about fifty times and you'll get some idea of what I'm up against. I'm trying to get my little brother into his page-boy outfit so that we won't be late for Dad's wedding, but I've been trying for the last hour without success.

Actually, I don't blame Rory for not wanting to put the suit on, but I'm not going to let him know that. And how am I going to get him to wear the pink silk sash that is supposed to go around his waist? I don't know what made Trish think that a seven-year-old boy was going to put up with that, but then everything was done in a bit of a hurry.

Trish and I had spent a whole afternoon at the fabric shop choosing the material for my dress. Eventually we picked a lovely cornflower-blue silk, because my eyes are blue. I couldn't wait for the dress to come and when I went to Dad's, on the weekend it was due, I was really excited. When Trish unpacked it and held it up for me to inspect, I was completely speechless.

"What do you think?" Trish asked me.

Instead of the beautiful blue silk, the dress was vile pink, and I don't think it was silk either but some fake nylon stuff. It wasn't even a nice pink, if there is such a thing. The only way I can think to describe it is Pig Pink. Obviously, it wasn't a mistake and they hadn't delivered the wrong dress or why would Trish be holding it up asking me what I thought? I couldn't tell her what I thought either, because this was Trish, not my mum, so I couldn't go off on to one and tell her that nothing in the world would make me wear that dress. Instead I just about managed not to cry and said, "What happened to the blue silk that we chose?"

"Oh, that turned out too expensive in the end and this gorgeous pink was on sale. Don't you like it?"

"It's lovely," I lied. I was trying to impress Trish with my mature attitude.

And now it's finally the day of the wedding and I really want to feel excited, but instead I'm just exasperated because I'm stuck with my annoying little brother. It's not fair.

"I want to wear this," says Rory, holding up his Spider-Man outfit.

I close my eyes, breathe in deeply, and count to ten. I assess my options. I could pin him down and force him into the suit, but then he'd start screaming and yelling and be totally uncooperative for the rest of the day. Alternatively, I could go and get Mum and insist that she deal with him, but I'm not actually talking to her at the moment so that could be a bit difficult. Or I could just give up and let him go to the wedding as Spider-Man. I decide to go for the fourth option: bribery.

"If you put the suit on I'll buy you that Pokémon comic you wanted."

"You mean this one," he says, picking it up from beside his bed. "Mum got it for me yesterday."

Just my luck. She's always spoiling him, which is why he's such a brat. I grab the comic off him and hold it high above my head.

"Okay. Put the suit on and I'll let you have it back."

He doesn't look impressed so I hold it by the spine, making a tiny rip. "And I won't tear it in half."

He picks up the pants off the floor. He knows I'm not joking. But he's not going to give up without a fight.

"I'll put these on if you read me a story tonight."

As you can see, my brother is no stranger to bribery.

"Okay." I hate reading to Rory, but all I want right now is for him to be ready when the taxi gets here.

"Promise you'll read me a story."

"I said okay, didn't I?"

He smiles triumphantly and scrambles into his pants. I sigh at the sight. They're all creased from being on the floor while we were arguing. Also, they're too short. He must have grown since Trish ordered them for him. Typical. Now we both look stupid.

At this point Mum sticks her head into the room. "You both look gorgeous."

Yeah, right!

"Rory, hurry up and get your jacket and shoes on. I have to go to work now. I'll see you later—have a wonderful time."

To my ears her cheerfulness sounds a bit forced. I don't think she likes the idea of Dad remarrying. Well, she should have thought about that before she left him. I have no sympathy for her whatsoever. Luckily, she doesn't seem to be expecting a reply—which is just as well.

I'm so relieved Rory's finally ready that I completely forget about the pink silk sash that's meant to go around his waist. It doesn't help that he's kicked it under the bed. He only tells me this when we're in the taxi and it's too late to do anything about it. If Trish notices, I'll blame it on Mum. I know that doesn't sound very nice, but it's important that I look good in front of Dad and Trish at the moment. You see, when they suddenly decided to get married and move out of their tiny apartment into a two-bedroom house, I came up with a brilliant plan. I just need the right moment to break it to them.

The taxi drops us off in town outside the registry office. When Dad and Trish told us they were getting married and said I could be a bridesmaid, the wedding suddenly became my favorite daydream.

I imagined myself walking up the aisle of a beautiful old church in the country. A big organ was playing "Wedding March" and every available surface was covered in white and pink flowers. The sun was coming through the stained-glass windows. In this dream, my boring straight hair (which Mum says is toffee colored and won't let me dye, even though it's obviously "beige") is transformed into a thick curtain of waving blonde gorgeousness. I am also willowy thin and zit-free. The wedding guests gasp as I walk down the aisle. One old lady nearly faints and has to be taken out into the churchyard to recover. When we reach the altar, the vicar, who is very young and very handsome, blushes when our eyes meet. At the reception, which is held in a very posh country house hotel, there is an endless stream of gorgeous boys waiting to dance with me. The photographers from *Hello!* magazine can't get enough of me either.

This daydream got me through countless math classes. Naturally, the reality couldn't have been further away from it. When Trish said they were having the wedding at the registry office, with the reception in a pub because their apartment is too small, my dream dissolved like wet cotton candy.

Of course, I tried to steer Trish away from her grotesque wedding plan. I even offered to organize it all for her, because she has a very exciting and time-consuming job and I thought that might be the reason why she wasn't concentrating on having The Wedding of the Year. As it turned out, it was because they wanted to get married as soon as possible and they'd only managed to get the registry office on that day because someone had canceled. Also, they couldn't afford anything grander, what with the move and everything.

I still tried to have the wedding daydream but it wasn't the same anymore. Mr. Green's voice kept infiltrating, droning on about fractions and stuff and drowning out the organ music, so in the end I gave up.

And now everything's turning out even worse than I thought it would. As we get out of the taxi, it starts to rain. I grab Rory and run to shelter in the nearest shop doorway, but not before some serious damage has been done to my hair, which I spent hours on this morning, trying to get it to curl. Now it's hanging in lank, wet snakes and my new silk pumps are soaked. Just to add to my problems, Rory begins to whine.

"Where's Dad? I thought he was going to meet us."

I have some sympathy with this. Where the hell *is* Dad? He said he'd be here. He couldn't bring us himself so he paid for a taxi to come and get us and drop us off at the registry office where, he'd said, he would be waiting. I scan the street, which isn't too crowded because of the rain, but I can't see Dad anywhere.

After about ten minutes, I'm seriously worried and fed up with having to stand out in the rain every time someone wants to go in or out of the shop. As we're sheltering in the doorway to a newsstand, this is pretty much all the time. By now Rory's whining has turned to complaining, and I'm very close to joining in. People are staring at us, which is hardly surprising, considering what we're wearing. I haven't brought a coat, so there's nothing to tone down the pink effect.

It suddenly occurs to me that I am stranded in a seedy part of town and I don't even have any money with me. In fact, all I have is a seven-year-old who is crying in earnest now and who is relying on *me* to do something. Perhaps I could call Mum except a) I'm not talking to her, and b) I don't have a cell phone. Ironically, this is the main reason that I'm not speaking to her. I've explained, till I'm blue in the face, that I'm the only fourteen-year-old in the *world* without a cell phone, but all she does is say, "Has Imogen got one?" to which I have to reply "No," because she hasn't.

It's no good trying to explain that Imogen, who by the way is my best friend, is a special case because it's hopeless trying to explain anything to Mum. She never listens and always ends the conversation with the extremely annoying sentence, "It's about time you realized that not everything is about you, Alice." This is *so* unfair because in her eyes *nothing* is about me, not one tiny little thing.

But back to the present dilemma and what to do, except I can't think straight because Rory is off again. "I want to go home. Why can't we go home?"

I try explaining that it's too far to walk home and anyway, nothing would persuade me to walk through town in this getup.

By now I'm seriously freezing. Who in their right mind has a wedding in February? So I go into the shop just to keep warm, even though I can't buy so much as a penny candy. It's blissfully warm inside, if a bit on the smelly side. It's one of those old newsstands that smell of wet dog and newspapers, which is hardly surprising really as that is exactly what's in here. The dog, which I assume belongs to the owner, goes some way to cheering Rory up. It's a big golden retriever and it goes up to him, wagging its tail, and slobbers all over him.

There's a woman behind the counter. She's talking to a customer, an old wrinkly man, and they both turn and stare at us.

"Well, well. Look what the dog dragged in." The old man's laugh is a painful-sounding wheeze. He thinks he's hilarious because Rory is being dragged across the shop by the dog, which is busy chewing the sleeve of his jacket. Luckily Rory doesn't seem to mind and he's actually laughing now, so I just leave them to get on with it.

"What can I get you?" The woman sounds very friendly and kind, but I can feel myself going bright red and can't think what to say.

Rory has none of my problems. He's never shy and can talk to anyone. He shakes off the dog, makes his eyes all big, and says to the lady in his best voice, "We've recently been orphaned and abandoned. We're all alone and have nowhere to live and were wondering if you could take us in and look after us. I've always wanted to live in a candy shop."

Rory's always doing this sort of thing. I think it's just to embarrass me, because he never does it when Mum's there. And the weird thing is that, whereas I find his behavior deeply annoying and puke-making, most adults think it's desperately cute and they go all gooey eyed and say, "Ahh, I'd love to have you, but—" at which point I always step in and save them the embarrassment of trying to think of an excuse. This is exactly what's happening now with the big shop lady, so I jump in and say, "We're looking for the registry office."

"You don't say! You're getting married, are you?" says the old man, going off into wheeze world again. "And there was me thinking you were the new bubblegum sales rep." He points at my hideous dress and he's so amused by this oh-so-funny joke that he goes into a paroxysm of laughter and I'm seriously worried that he might actually die.

I ignore him, but Rory, who's just got the joke, is now dancing around me shouting, "Bubblegum, bubblegum," over and over. That's the trouble with seven-year-olds; they never know when to stop.

"Now, let me see," says the shop lady. "There used to be a registry office two doors down, but they've just moved it, haven't they, Stan?" She appeals to the old man, who's just about recovered his breath.

"Yep, it's a travel agent now. You could book your honeymoon there." And he's off again, overcome by his own wit.

"So where is it now?" I manage, through gritted teeth. "We're missing our dad's wedding." I'm close to tears, because I've just realized that they'll all be waiting for us and won't have a clue where we are.

"I think they moved it to the town hall," says Stan gleefully and he's about to start his wheezy laugh again but the shop lady, seeing a tear finally escape and mingle with the rain on my face, gives him a warning look.

"Here, I'll draw you a map. It shouldn't take you more than fifteen minutes, if you walk quickly." She hastily scribbles some lines on a paper bag and holds it out to me, smiling encouragingly. I grab it with one hand and Rory with the other, and yelling "Thank you," we run.

The run soon slows to a trot, and then a walk. Although it's not raining heavily anymore, it is mizzling—a sort of cross between drizzle and mist, which you walk through without realizing how wet you're actually getting. Of course, Rory is whining again. "Why can't we get in another taxi?" His whiny voice really gets on my nerves.

"Yeah, right," I say. "And God knows where we'd end up then. We might get the same stupid taxi driver and he'd probably drop us at the zoo or something."

"The zoo, the zoo! I want to go to the zoo. Let's go to the zoo, Alice. It's much better than a boring old wedding."

Aaarrgh. I really want to hit my little brother sometimes. Well, nearly all the time, actually. The trouble is, if I do, he'll start bawling and we're just entering the center of town where all the shops are, and I'm desperately trying to keep a low profile. If anyone from school sees me in this dress I think I will literally die. Oh, God! What if I bumped into Sasha and her friends?

And then, of course, because this is my life we're talking about, that is exactly what happens. I see Sasha coming out of Accessorize, surrounded by her horrible friends. I just freeze. I go hot and then cold. She hasn't seen me yet because she's showing off a new pair of earrings. Even though they're all too far away to hear, I can imagine her friends going, "Ooh, Sasha. They do suit you." That'll be Chelsea. And Clara will be saying, "Oh, Sash, are you going to wear them to your party?" She's been going on about her fifteenth birthday party for weeks and how wonderful it's going to be.

She's still admiring herself in the shop window so I dive for cover into the nearest shop.

"Are we here? Is this it? Where's Dad?"

God! Why is my brother so thick? This is so obviously a bookshop. Rory is hopeless at reading, which is probably why he's always trying to get me to read to him.

I look at the map. The town hall is at the end of this street. I peer out of the doorway and see Sasha and company going into Starbucks. That is so typical of her. When I come shopping in town with Imogen, we always go into the café near the station because it's about four times cheaper. And we go to Claire's instead of Accessorize for the same reason. Not that we shop that often, because I've never got any money and Imogen doesn't like shopping much. She says it's boring, which of course it is, if you haven't got any money.

Finally we make it to the town hall and, miracle of miracles, there's Dad standing under the portico looking worriedly up and down the street.

"Where the hell have you been?" He looks seriously stressed out. Well, he's not the only one. I'm just about to launch into an explanation about the hopeless taxi driver and the rain and the newsstand and the trek across town, when Trish appears.

"Thank God!" she says. "There you are. Come on, let's go." Instead of heading into the building, they set off up the road, me and Rory dragging along behind like pieces of luggage. It's then that I realize that Trish is not wearing her long, white, dreamy wedding dress. Instead, she's got on a very smart but, let's face it, very boring cream-colored suit. I hurry to catch up with her.

"Why aren't you wearing your dress? What about the wedding?" I realize I sound painfully like Rory with his interminable questions, but it can't be helped.

"You've missed the wedding. We couldn't wait forever. We were lucky to get that slot in the first place. As it was we held on as long as possible and then the registrar had to hurry the ceremony because the next group was waiting."

"But your lovely dress, why aren't you wearing it?" My voice comes out a bit squeaky.

"I never had time to finish it." Trish's voice is tight and I realize that she, too, is seriously stressed. What's wrong with everyone? I thought weddings were supposed to be happy occasions. "Anyhow," she continues as we approach an extremely seedy-looking pub, "there didn't seem much point when I realized that your dad wasn't going to rent a *smart* suit."

I look at Dad who is indeed looking like he always does, in one of his sad work suits.

Trish hasn't finished yet. "I decided I'd look hopelessly overdressed, so I just put on my best conference suit."

"Great. Well, thanks for telling me!" I desperately want to say, but I don't trust myself to speak without blubbing.

Chapter Two

I can't believe it. I spent all morning trying to get Rory into his suit, when frankly he'd have been better off in his Spider-Man outfit. At least now I'm not the only one at the party in fancy dress. Not only have I been totally humiliated in this disastrous dress, I never even got to be a bridesmaid because we missed the bloody wedding. I know my face is bright red from all the pent-up fury, injustice, disappointment, embarrassment, and about a hundred other emotions that seem to be coursing through my veins at this moment. No doubt it's clashing horribly with the pink.

Dad is at the bar ordering a round of drinks. I go and stand next to him and make the mistake of leaning on the counter. There's about a century's worth of old sticky beer, which I thought was varnish, and I have to peel my arm off in a hurry. There's nothing to wipe it on. The man next to my dad is grinning at me in a slightly creepy manner and I'm just thinking it would be best to ignore him when he hands me a big white handkerchief. I smile with relief and wipe my arm clean.

"Hello. I'm Terry."

I'm trying to surreptitiously sidle closer to Dad so that he can rescue me from this weirdo, but Dad's eyes are fixed on the TV above the bar. The afternoon racing's on and I can tell from the way he's standing—sort of all tense—that he's got a bet on. When the race finishes his shoulders slump, he thrusts his hands into his pockets, and I know that he hasn't won.

Trish thinks that Dad has given up gambling and he even had me convinced for a while. But I know my dad. What other reason could there be for choosing such a dive to hold a wedding reception in, other than it's next to a bookies and it shows the racing on the TV? Trish must have been born yesterday.

I give Dad a quick hug to cheer him up. I hope he didn't lose too much.

"Enjoying yourself, Princess?" he says, hugging me back.

I know I'm too old for such names but I still love it when he calls me that. It gives me a warm feeling inside. I wish he'd made more of an effort and worn a smarter suit, though. Never mind, he's so handsome he'd look good in a sack and boots.

Terry is still lurking and grinning at me. I can hardly say to Dad, "There's some old perv trying to chat me up," when said perv is standing right next to me, so I just stand there blushing, as usual, and tug on Dad's sleeve because he's still glued to the racing. Eventually, Dad turns around and sees the old man.

"Alice, this is Terry." Great. Now he's introducing me to the nutter. "This is Trisha's father. Your new step-grandfather, I suppose," he says cheerfully.

The thought that I might have grandparents, albeit step ones, is giving me a funny feeling. You see, I don't have any grandparents. Dad's mum and dad are both dead. I used to have a gran, my mum's mum, but she died a few years ago.

"We've already met," says Terry, tucking his now sticky hanky into his trouser pocket. "I shall escort the young lady into dinner," and he takes my arm and leads me over to the tables in the corner of the pub. They've been pushed together—a bit awkwardly as they're round—and they've got handwritten *Reserved* signs on them.

"Before we sit down and get acquainted, I'd better introduce you to Trisha's mother—only whatever you do, don't call her Granny," he says, laughing.

When Terry finally manages to locate his wife, in a gaggle of women all crowded around Trish—her work mates, no doubt—I can see why he thought this was so funny. She's even more glamorous than Trish and looks more like her sister than her mother.

"Joan, this is Alice," says Terry, and I'm waiting for the bit about me being her new step-granddaughter and maybe her hugging me, but he doesn't say it so I just smile weakly. Joan is staring at me and I'm suddenly aware of how damp and bedraggled I must look.

"You know, Gary's daughter," Terry points out. This information still doesn't raise a smile from her so Terry adds, somewhat obviously, "She's Trisha's bridesmaid."

"Patricia didn't have any bridesmaids." Trish's mum says this accusingly, glaring at us both, and I want to say, "What—do you think I'd dress like this for fun?" and then think it might be better to explain about the misdirected taxi and the mad dash across town, but I don't get a chance because Joan has turned her attention toward her husband.

"Honestly, Terry. I can't take you anywhere. What's happened to your handkerchief?" She's pointing at the breast pocket of his suit.

"Oh, that," says Terry innocently. "I'm glad you put that there, it came in very handy just now," and he turns and winks at me.

"That handkerchief was purely for decorative effect, Terence. It was not supposed to be *used*." Tutting loudly, she turns back to Trish.

Come to think of it, Dad has canceled our weekend with him on more than one occasion because they've had to go and see Trish's parents. I used to feel resentful and wondered why we couldn't go as well. Now I can see that Dad was sparing us, rather than excluding us.

"Sorry about that," says Terry as we go to sit down. "She's upset. This isn't really the kind of wedding she had in mind for her only daughter."

No, and I don't suppose Dad was the sort of man she had in mind for a son-in-law. She probably thinks that Dad's too old for her daughter, and he's divorced and has two children already. Not exactly Catch of the Year. I think Terry knows what I'm thinking because he takes a swig of his beer and nods toward Dad, who's standing at the bar telling a joke. Everyone around him is laughing and smacking him on the back.

"Great guy, your dad. Trisha's a lucky girl." Terry grins.

I'm so grateful, I could kiss him.

Although I feel a bit awkward talking to Terry, I'm really glad that he's sitting with me because there's no one here that I know, and if it wasn't for my new step-grandad I'd be sitting all alone. Dad's showing Rory how to use the slot machine, even though it's got a huge sign on it saying: *You must be over 18 to play on this machine.* Sometimes I suspect that my dad might be a bit irresponsible.

I find myself telling Terry all about my disastrous day and he thinks it's hilarious and is laughing at it all, but in a nice way, so I don't mind and eventually even I start to see the funny side.

"Well," he says when I've finished, "I think you look lovely in that dress." He's pushing it a bit there, but I let him off. "And not at all like a piece of bubblegum. More like a yummy iced bun," he adds, winking at me, and I slap him on the arm.

"Seriously, though," he says, looking all serious, "I do think that you were very mature and sensible, managing to find the right place and looking after your little brother." This has me blushing bright red again, but thankfully everyone's coming to sit down now for the meal.

I had expected there to be some special food prepared, but Dad is handing menus around that he's picked up off the bar.

"Have anything you want," he informs everyone cheerfully, "it's all on me." Joan looks thunderous and I can see that Trish is close to tears. Even Terry looks a bit embarrassed and I suddenly feel like sticking up for my dad. I know he's doing his best, and if it doesn't come up to Trish's standards, well, she should have organized it better. Even I could have organized a better wedding than this, for heaven's sake. Why did it all have to be done in such a rush, anyway? They've been living together for about seven years, it's not as if they even needed to get married.

Of course, the food takes ages to arrive, and it doesn't all come at once so some people finish before some have even started. My scampi and chips are nearly the last to appear and now Terry is talking to Dad, so I daydream my number one daydream of the moment, which is all the more exciting because there's a chance that this one might actually happen.

It goes like this: When Dad and Trish move out of their tiny flat and into their new house, which has *two* bedrooms, they ask me if I would like to move in with them. Of course Rory can't come, because he's too young and ought to stay with Mum. They buy a lovely house, which is near to my school so I can walk there in the morning and don't have to go on the bus anymore. The house has got a huge attic bedroom with its own connected bathroom, with a whirlpool bath and shower and a brilliant view of the park from the window. Okay. This is stretching the truth a bit, because there's no way Trish and Dad would let me have this room—I'd probably get the storage room—and there's no park near our school, but who cares, this is my daydream. Before I move in, Dad takes me to Ikea and says I can have anything I like, so I wander around all the lovely rooms that they have set up in there and choose something fun yet sophisticated. I choose the curtains and the duvet cover and the towels to match to go in the bathroom. While I'm doing this Dad goes off to buy me a computer to have on the desk that stretches right across one wall. When he comes back, he's really pleased and says that the shop was doing this really good deal and he got a flat-screen TV and a PlayStation as well.

After my room is finished, Trish comes in and opens the wardrobe and says, "Oh dear, I think we'd better go shopping for some new clothes."

And then, instead of taking me to all the boring shops in town, we go to the city and spend hours shopping and have to go back to the car three times with our bags because Trish has let me have anything I want. Then we have coffee in one of those coffee shops with the sofas instead of chairs.

I'm really getting into this daydream and just wondering if perhaps my room has its own staircase that comes up from the garden onto its own balcony, when I'm brought back down to earth by Dad, who's standing up and tapping his beer glass with his knife.

"I want to thank you all for coming today," he says. "I won't make a long speech." Thank God for that, I think, because I can tell that he's slightly drunk. "I'd just like to say that today Trish has made me the happiest man alive." Trish manages a smile, just. "But before I sit down I must thank the bridesmaid and page boy"—he's grinning at me and Rory—"and I hope that my daughter isn't as late for her own wedding as she was for mine."

Late! What is he talking about? I missed it! Everyone is sniggering politely and, of course, I've gone bright red again. "Anyway," Dad continues, "here is a small token to show my appreciation," and he's getting two parcels from under the table: a huge one for Rory and a tiny one for me.

Rory rips the paper off his parcel immediately. Inside is a remote-control monster truck, which of course he wants to use straight away and can't because it hasn't got any batteries in it. Terry averts the inevitable tantrum by taking him out to the nearest shop to buy some and promising to let him play with it in the pub garden. I breathe a sigh of relief. That would usually be my job.

I hate opening presents in front of people, especially when life has taught me not to get my hopes up. So I wait for everyone to start talking again before opening mine.

I stroke the shiny paper that my parcel is wrapped in. I know it's customary for the groom to give the bridesmaids some sort of jewelry at weddings, a locket or something, and I'm hoping Dad got Trish to choose it because he's hopeless at that sort of thing.

I glance over at her to see if she's watching, so that I can smile at her when I open it. She's staring at me across the room and I'm shocked at the look she gives me. It's horrid—all mean and spiteful. Then she turns away to talk to her mother, and I convince myself that I was imagining it. I open the box and lift the tissue paper and there, nestling underneath, is a cell phone.

I manage to ignore the fact that it's pink. Why do people think that girls want everything to be pink? I hate pink, especially after today. But who cares what color it is. The point is, I've got a cell phone at last.

Dad's there beside me. "Thanks, Dad. It's brilliant," I say, and I give him a big kiss.

"Only the best for my girl." He's nearly as pleased as I am.

I can't help worrying though about how much it cost him. And Rory's monster truck can't have been cheap either.

"It's got plenty of minutes on it. You just let me know when it runs out and I'll top it up for you."

I give him another hug. He really is the best dad in the world.

Chapter Three

Dad calls a taxi to take us home because he's been drinking and can't drive us back himself. The hall light is on, but when I open the door I know Mum's not there because the house feels empty. There's a note stuck on the fridge door.

Dear Alice,

Sorry, had to go back into work. I shouldn't be too long, but if I'm not back by 7:30 please make sure Rory gets to bed.

Love, Mum

I look at the clock above the stove and it's eight-thirty. This happens all the time. She's always "having to run into work."

While I've been reading the note, Rory has turned all the lights on downstairs and the television and now he's racing his truck up and down the hallway. He hasn't quite got the hang of the controls yet and it keeps bumping into the baseboard, leaving great big dents. This doesn't worry me particularly, because basically our house is a dump. The hall floor is wooden, but not the sort of wooden floor you see in magazines, which have been laid and are all flat and polished and smart. Ours is just the floorboards, which are all dusty and spattered with paint. Mum pulled the linoleum up years ago and said, "Look at those lovely floorboards. They'll come out great when they've been sanded and waxed." Only they never have been.

We used to live in a lovely house. By "we" I mean Mum and Dad and me. Then when Rory was born, Mum threw Dad out and we had to sell the house and me and Mum and Rory had to move. We couldn't afford to buy another house so Mum rented this one—which is truly horrible. I don't know what she was thinking when she chose to live here. It belongs to an old lady, Miss

Maybrooke—a friend of Mum's, who was moving into a nursing home down the road. Mum said we had to have it because the rent was so cheap. Well, of course it is—the place is a dump.

Mum said we'd just have to make the best of it and when she'd fixed it up, it would be fine. The only problem is she never has fixed it up because, she says, she hasn't got the time or the money. As a result, most of the things in the house are really old-fashioned and might look all right if you're about ninety years old with very bad eyesight. The front room has got a gas fire in it, which smells even when it's not on. The walls are covered in really hideous wallpaper, all green and brown. Mum says it looks Victorian and might actually be original. She says this in a sort of awed voice, as if that should mean we can't paint over it or something. So what if it's Victorian. It doesn't make it nice.

Miss Maybrooke left some of her furniture behind and Mum says we have to keep it because it's not ours to dispose of and there's nowhere else for it to go. It's all big and heavy and made out of dark wood. When I was younger, it used to scare me, the way it sort of loomed over me. Now it just irritates me because it makes the rooms feel cramped and dark.

The only room that isn't completely hideous is the kitchen. Mum did get a bit of money when they sold the old house and she used it to remodel the kitchen. It can look nice when Mum bothers to clean it up. At the moment, all the breakfast things are piled in the sink and there's a puddle of milk on the table (where Rory sits, of course).

Unfortunately, there wasn't enough money left over to do the bathroom as well. Mum says that Miss Maybrooke was very proud of the bathroom because she had redone it. But that was way back in the 1970s when, according to Mum, an "avocado" bathroom was all the rage. So now we have to put up with a sludge green tub, sink, and toilet.

Sometimes I feel like I'm living in a museum, but mostly I feel as though I'm living in someone else's house, so I never really feel at home.

I'm dying to be alone with my new phone, so I take it up to my bedroom. First of all I have to get out of this dress. The relief when I've got it off and put my pajamas on is bliss. I get the phone out of the box and look at it. To be honest, I'm a bit scared of it. We don't have a lot of high-tech things in this house. We haven't even got a microwave, let alone a computer or a PlayStation. We've got a television but it's not a flat-screen one or anything fancy and we can only get five channels on it.

I decide to work out as much as I can about the phone by fiddling around with it, because the instruction book looks even scarier than the phone. I manage to get into the phone book and work out how to list people's numbers. I start off with our home number, which I list under *Mum*, then I put in Dad's number at the flat and wish that I'd asked him and Trish for their cell phone numbers. If Imogen would get a phone then we could text each other all the time—it would be great. She says there's no point in her having one because there's absolutely no one she wants to talk to. Perhaps she'll change her mind now I've got one.

I can't believe I've only got two numbers to enter so I put in Mrs. Archer's number. She lives down the road and picks Rory up from school when Mum's working. I usually have to collect him from her on my way home. After that I really can't think of any more numbers I might need and I suddenly feel a bit depressed, sort of like *having* the phone isn't half as exciting as *wanting* it.

It might be different if there was someone who could show me how it worked properly. The camera on it is great, though, and I look around for something I can take a picture of.

I hate my room—like the rest of the house, it doesn't really feel like mine. Even though I stick posters and postcards all over the walls it still manages to look like I'm camping out in some-one's guest bedroom. It's a complete dump. There are clothes all over the floor and most of the drawers are hanging open. Mum's always nagging me to clean it up, but I can't see the point. It's hor-rible, anyway, whether I tidy it up or not.

The best thing in here is the strings of lights I bought once when I went to Ikea with Mum. They're hung all around my head board (you guessed it, it's big and dark and Victorian), and all around the fireplace. This is a big old fireplace. It's got tiles down the side, which I quite like because they've got a blue and gold leaf pattern all over them. Other than that it's useless and I have to stuff newspaper up it to stop the drafts and so that birds don't fall down the chimney and end up in my room.

In the end, I point the camera at myself, but because I'm concentrating so hard on how it works I forget to smile and the flash goes off and the picture of me comes out looking like a ghost. A frightened, depressed ghost. I'm just fiddling around looking for the delete option when I hear a crash from downstairs. Damn, I forgot about Rory. It's quarter to ten and he should have been in bed hours ago. Mum will probably be home any minute and I'll be in serious trouble.

When I get downstairs it's ominously quiet. I push the door of the living room open and peer inside. I can tell immediately what has happened, despite the fact it looks as though a small bomb has gone off. Rory has taken the throw off the sofa and tried to construct a tent with it between the sofa and the table. In order to stop it from slipping off the polished surface of the table, he has piled anything he could find on top of the table. Several heaps of books and DVDs, plus a couple of chairs and a lamp, are now lying on the floor with the throw crumpled up beneath them. There is a suspicious-looking, Rory-sized lump beneath all of this.

"Rory, get out of there immediately." I am aware of how like my mother I sound and hate myself for it.

The lump doesn't move.

"Rory, NOW."

Still nothing. For one glorious moment I entertain the fantasy that Rory is dead. I gloss over the fact that I will be blamed and that my mother will be in trouble for leaving a fourteen-year-old in charge of a seven-year-old, and fast forward to the funeral, where I look stunning in black and have to be supported by one of the young, handsome coffin bearers as a few artfully arranged tears roll down my pale but flawless cheeks without smudging my waterproof mascara at all.

This may seem a bit harsh, but let me explain. If it wasn't for Rory my life would not have fallen apart. Mum would still be the old Mum that she was before he was born and she might not have thrown Dad out.

You see, after Rory was born, Mum suffered from really bad postnatal depression. It was so bad that some days she never even got out of bed. Gran was still alive then, and she did her best to look after us, but she had enough on her plate with Mum, so I had to help out a lot by looking after Rory. Gran used to joke that my little brother was well named and that it should have been spelled Roary instead.

All Rory ever seemed to do was scream, and it was usually my job to make him stop. I'd go into his room and see him in his crib, his ugly red face even redder and uglier than normal, all scrunched up in a scream, and somehow I'd have to stop him. Picking him up and rocking him was no good because it just made him scream all the louder. I discovered that if I picked up his toys and made them walk along the edge of the crib and gave them funny voices then he stopped crying. I'd start by making the voice quiet so that if he wanted to hear it he'd have to stop making a noise.

As he got older and had one of those cribs with bars and could sit up and look out, I discovered that if I took all my toys into his room and played with them on the floor in front of his crib that usually kept him quiet for hours. I'd take all my Barbie dolls in there and play out stories with them. It was a bit like being at the theater for him. He had the best front-row seat and I got to play everyone from the princess to the prince and the evil witch. Of course he didn't really know what was going on, so I could make anything up as long as I made them have funny voices and made them move around a lot.

This worked quite well until Rory was about two. By then

Mum was getting better and not relying on me so much. But then Gran died and Mum got bad again for about a year. If she was in bed having a nap, it was up to me to keep Rory quiet.

The problem was that the old game of him watching me play didn't work anymore. Now he wanted to play as well, but his idea of fun was to stuff my Barbie dolls into his slobbery mouth, rip their limbs from their bodies, and stick their feet up his nose. Those were the darkest days, but I managed to convince myself that, as I was nearly ten, I was getting too old for them, anyway.

Then last year Mum got a job at the old people's home, or nursing home I should say, where Miss Maybrooke is. It's only at the end of our road, which Mum thought would be great because she wouldn't need to drive there and she'd be on hand if we needed her. Unfortunately, all it means is that when they're short staffed, which seems to me to be all the time, they call on my mum because she lives so close and she says she can't say no, because the boss gets funny with her if she does, and cuts her hours down. I can't help thinking that Mum is a chump to play into his hands in this way and she should tell him what's what. Anyhow, it means that she's never here anymore and it's up to me to look after Rory again.

So I hope you can see that my fantasy wasn't that harsh after all and that if Rory wasn't here my life would be drastically improved. That's why I conceived the Plan I was talking about earlier, where I go and live with Dad and Trish and can lead a civilized and peaceful existence. Which reminds me, I forgot to mention it to Dad at the wedding. I've been trying to find the right moment for ages now. I will definitely do it next time I see him.

I make a halfhearted attempt at picking up some of the things that are all over the floor. Rory's schoolbag has burst open and his tatty books are littered about. As I pick up his literacy book, it falls open and catches my eye because at the top of the page it says *My Big Sister*. His homework was to write an essay on me! I can't resist reading it.

My big sister is big and scary.

The cheek! I'll give him scary! I read on.

She shouts a lot and she doesn't like me much. I wish I had a little sister then I could shout at her. I like it when she reads me stories but she never does. She is mean and she smells pooey.

That's the thanks I get, after all I do for him! I see with some satisfaction that the teacher wasn't too impressed either. She's circled the word *pooey* and written, *This is not a nice word, Rory.*

Rory has gotten bored with playing dead and comes out from under the chaos. I stuff the book back into his schoolbag.

"Quick," I tell him, "get into bed before Mum gets back."

"Never," he says defiantly.

"You'll be in trouble."

"You mean you'll be in trouble," he says, giving me a sly grin so I feel like hitting him. Unfortunately he's got me on that one. Mum will be cross with me for not getting him into bed and he knows it, which makes my job all the more difficult.

"You said you'd read me a story," he whines. "I'll go if you read me a story."

"Don't be bloody ridiculous, it's far too late," I say. There is nothing I hate more than reading Rory a story. And I'm certainly not going to read him one after what he wrote about me.

"But you promised!" He's folded his arms now and stuck out his bottom lip. The next stage is a full-blown tantrum.

"I never promised," I yell back at him.

"You did, too."

"Didn't."

"Did."

This could go on for hours, and sometimes does, because I want to see who is the first to crack, even though it's usually me; Rory can go on all day. I decide I've had enough already so I grab him by the arm and drag him into the hall and, of course, he starts screaming so I don't hear the key in the lock as Mum lets herself in.

"For God's sake, Alice. Why isn't he in bed? It's ten o'clock! He's not even in his pajamas."

Great. Here we go.

"Is it really too much to ask? I've just done a twelve-hour shift and I have to come home to this."

I let go of Rory's arm and he runs, blubbering, to Mum who gives him a big hug.

"She hurt me," he wails, and Mum gives me that awful disappointed look.

"You're lucky I didn't kill you," I yell.

"She promised she'd read me a story and now she won't. *And* she swore at me."

"Enough," says Mum. She looks at Rory. "You go upstairs and get into your pajamas and brush your teeth and then Alice will come up and read you a story."

"Mum!" I yell as Rory gives me a triumphant smile and scurries upstairs. "That is *so* unfair."

"Don't start," says Mum firmly. "If you made a promise, you must keep it."

"But I didn't." My voice is getting more shrill, but I can't help it. She hasn't even asked about the wedding.

"Stop arguing and just do as you're told for once."

"Why is it always me that has to do as I'm told? Why can't Rory do as he's told?" I scream back. I can't remember the last time I had a normal conversation with my mother where one or the other of us wasn't shouting. Then I remember that I'm not even meant to be speaking to her.

Just then Rory, now in his pajamas, comes shooting down the stairs.

"Mum, look what Dad gave me." He retrieves the monster truck from behind the umbrella stand and shoves it at Mum.

"Very nice," she says, but I can see her lips pursing and I know exactly what she's thinking, even though she'd never say it to Rory. She's calculating what it will cost to buy new batteries when these run out, and thinking how thoughtless Dad is to buy him such a present.

"He bought Alice a cell phone," pipes up Rory. Mum's mouth

goes so thin at this news that her lips practically disappear. She glares at me.

"What?" I say as nonchalantly as possible.

"Is that true?" she asks.

She looks really upset. I know exactly what she's thinking. She's thinking, if Dad can afford to give me such an expensive present, how come he can't afford to pay her more child support and why does he keep missing payments? Of course she'll never say this out loud because she never bad-mouths Dad in front of us. Not that that makes any difference when I can tell what she's thinking. She should give Dad a break. After all, he spent the money on us, which is more than she ever does. Hence our long-running argument about the cell phone.

"Yes, he did," I reply. "And it's just as well, because I could really have used it this morning." Damn, too late I realize what I've said. I wasn't going to tell Mum about going to the wrong place and missing the wedding.

Mum is busy taking off her coat and getting her slippers on and I think I might have got away with it, but of course I'd forgotten about Rory and his big mouth.

"We got lost and then we got wet and had to run and then we had to hide from some bad people and we never saw the wedding. We just went to the pub instead."

Thanks, Rory. Now Mum's going to think that Dad is totally incompetent and if I'm not careful she might not let him look after us at weekends. Not that we've been to see him much lately. He's had so much to work on.

"It wasn't a big deal," I say airily. "The taxi driver didn't know that the registry office had been moved to the town hall, that's all. If I'd had a phone I could have rung Dad, and he could have come and got us." I've definitely scored a point there, I think.

"No, he couldn't, silly. He was getting married," Rory points out.

"Whatever." I shrug and go into the kitchen.

I still can't believe we missed Dad's wedding. He finally finds a lovely woman that he wants to spend the rest of his life with and we miss the big moment. Suddenly I feel like crying. I flop down into a chair and rest my head on the table and think about what an awful day it's been. My peace is soon shattered when Mum and Rory come into the kitchen.

"I'm hungry," wails Rory. "I want something to eat."

"What did you have for tea?" she asks us. There's a silence while I think. We haven't had anything to eat since lunchtime, which seems an awfully long time ago now.

"We didn't have anything," pipes up Rory.

Mum gives me The Look.

"It's not my fault. We've only just got home."

"No, we haven't. We've been home ages. I built a den but Alice ruined it and buried me under a pile of books and stuff. I could hardly breathe. I thought I was going to die." Rory is always exaggerating and tries to make me look bad whenever he can.

"That is such a lie." I take a swipe at him across the table because I know that Mum always believes him over me.

"Stop it, you two," says Mum. "I'm too tired for this. I'm going to make us some scrambled eggs on toast and then we'll all go to bed."

While she shuffles around the kitchen, Rory tells her all about the day, and I can tell by the way she is bashing the eggs to death in the bowl that she doesn't really want to hear about Dad's wedding. Well, it's her fault for throwing him out. In fact, the thought of that makes me so cross I decide to chip in.

"They had the reception in a really lovely pub," I tell her.

"Oh," says Mum, "which one was that?"

"I can't remember what it was called," I say.

"I can," says Rory, "it was called the King's Head. I remember because Terry told me that there used to be a picture outside of a king who had his head chopped off. But Terry said people complained because it was too gory. There was blood and stuff coming out of it—" He would have carried on if Mum hadn't interrupted.

"The King's Head! What, the one in the middle of town?"

I don't say anything, because I don't want Dad to look bad, but it's too late.

"He actually had a wedding reception in there?"

"Yes," said Rory. "It was great. We watched the racing and I played on the slot machine."

Mum's lips are pursed up again, but she just sighs and gives me that look again. As if it was my fault! I've had enough. I get up so quickly that my chair falls over. I don't care, I leave it where it is and shout, "It was a lovely wedding and Dad looked so handsome and Trish was really happy and everyone had a brilliant time," then I flounce out of the kitchen and run up to my bedroom.

When I'm alone I start crying, I don't know why. I pick up the pink dress that I left in a heap on the floor but instead of putting it in the laundry basket I stuff it into the wastepaper basket—but only after I've blown my nose on it. Then I crawl into bed and pull the duvet right up over my head and try to imagine that I'm somewhere else and some*one* else.

Chapter Four

I'm standing at the bus stop waiting for the school bus. This has definitely got to be the worst part of the day for me. Well, this and the bus home. There's only one other person from my school who catches the bus from this stop and that's a boy from Year Eight, so we ignore each other. As the bus comes around the bend and pulls up at the bus stop, I curse the fact that it's a single-decker bus. I do this every morning. If it was a double decker I could get away from Sasha and her cronies. But as it is, by the time the bus gets to my stop, she is sitting halfway up the aisle and the front of the bus is full of boys from Years Seven and Eight so I have to go past her to get a seat.

Every day Sasha makes it her mission to embarrass me in some way. She used to make fun of me because Mum wouldn't let me out of the house without my coat on. It was no good explaining to her that *nobody* wears a coat (except a few geeky boys) and that by making me wear one she was literally ruining my life. Then I hit on the solution of getting a bigger knapsack and hiding my coat in the bottom of it. Now Mum is willing to accept that I have one of those raincoats that packs up into a small bag, which I keep in the bottom of my bag, "for emergencies." Of course, there is no emergency on earth that would force me to actually wear the thing, but Mum lives under the illusion that if it was raining hard I would get it out and put it on.

So far it's been at the bottom of my knapsack for over a year and is covered in specks of melted chocolate, and is sticky at one end where a banana gunked all over it because I forgot it was in my bag and I didn't find it until it had gone black and split. So, anyway, Sasha stopped teasing me about my coat and took to tripping me up as I went past and then saying, "Ooh look, it's Alice in Blunderland." Everyone laughs of course, not because it's funny but because everyone always laughs when Sasha does something cruel. I think they're relieved it's not them she's picking on. Sasha has a way of saying things that seems to require a reaction, like she's playing to an audience.

I steel myself for what she has in store today. As I walk past her she says, very loudly so that even the Sixth Formers at the back of the bus look up, "Oh, look, it's The Virgin Alice."

I know I'm blushing and that everyone is staring and giggling and I hate her so much and I hate myself for blushing and probably looking like I'm about to cry, but I can't help it. I stumble as far down the bus as I dare without entering the Sixth-Form zone. I sit down in the nearest available seat and pretend to be looking for something in my bag, because I daren't look up and catch anyone's eye.

My red face is just subsiding and my heart is returning to its normal rhythm when the person I have sat down next to leans over and says, "You should just ignore her, you know."

I look around and once again the blood rushes to my cheeks and my heart goes mad again. I'm sitting next to one of the Sixth Form boys. What's he doing sitting this far forward? I've never seen him before—he must be new. I mean, he's not the sort of person you could miss. He's absolutely gorgeous. His hair is longer than most of the boys and it's caramel colored. He's got blue-gray eyes and no zits. And he's talking to *me*. Then I remember that only a few minutes ago the whole bus was sniggering because Sasha had called me a virgin, and I want the floor to open up and swallow me.

I spend the rest of the journey trying to look busy, checking my schedule and stuff, but I can see, out of the corner of my eye, that the boy is watching me the whole time.

Eventually he leans toward me and says, "Are we going to sit here all day? Not that I'd mind if I could sit next to you, but I think we should go into school. This is only my second day and I don't want to blot my school record this early in my academic career."

I realize that the bus has stopped and everyone is piling off, until only the Sixth Formers are left. One of them—Ryan I think he's called, he's in the sporty set—says, "Are you coming, Seth, or what?" I realize that I'm blocking the boy in, so I hurriedly get up and go down the bus. I can feel him behind me, and I try to hold on to the memory of his fresh, lemony aftershave, which made me almost giddy when he leaned toward me. As I climb off the bus, I'm dying to turn and get another look at him, but daren't. Then I feel his hand on my arm.

"See you around," he says, and he disappears with a group of boys into the Sixth Form block.

I hurry into our classroom so I can tell Imogen about him. Imogen always gets to school before me and sure enough there she is, sitting at her desk, in the corner at the back, reading a book.

The form is divided into groups. At the moment they're all hanging around because our teacher hasn't arrived yet. Basically there are the boys, who keep to themselves, except a few of them who are slightly more mature than the rest and fancy themselves ladies' men and try and flirt with some of the girls. The girls are split into roughly three groups. At the bottom of the heap are the no-hopers. These are the girls who are hopelessly geeky and don't care what they look like. They mostly have zits and greasy hair and still wear socks. I know this sounds awful, but it's just the way it is. Generally this lot don't get bullied because it's too easy and they're below the radar of someone like Sasha, who wouldn't deign to even look at them. Next are the girls that I think of as normal. Some of them verge on the geeky, they do their work and wear the right uniform, and some aspire to the other group, the group that is headed by Sasha.

Sasha's group sees itself as the pinnacle of everything. If you're not in her group you don't exist, unless you're being made fun of. Imogen refers to them as the "Handbag Brigade" because they actually come to school with handbags instead of schoolbags. They all wear as much makeup as they think they can get away with and they like to pretend not to do any work.

And then there's Imogen, who doesn't fit into any of these categories and so, by association, neither do I.

Imogen sees me coming and puts the book away. I'm glad because I suspect that, deep down, she'd rather carry on reading it. Let me explain Imogen to you and what it is about her that sets her apart. For starters, she's got a completely different hairstyle from everyone else. Most of the girls have their hair long and straighten it. Some, like Sasha and her gang, even have streaky highlights in theirs. Imogen has her hair, which is quite thick and almost black, cut into a style. It's like a bob, only it's shorter at the back and comes down into points at the front. It looks really grown up and it suits her because she's very mature in some ways. She doesn't seem to care what anyone thinks of her. Some of the girls are a bit wary of her because, if provoked, she can be sharp tongued, though not in a catty, personal way like Sasha, so people tend to leave her alone, including Sasha, and she likes it that way.

Imogen is good at every subject, though not in a geeky way. It's just the way she is. She dresses differently as well. Most girls wear their skirts really short and go around all day with the top two, and sometimes three, buttons of their blouses undone. Of course, we have to wear school uniform and ours is deadly dull and boring: black skirt or pants, white blouse, gray sweater, and a black blazer. I suppose it's better than St. Winifred's uniform, though. They have to wear purple and green tartan skirts and purple blazers.

Anyhow, Imogen looks completely different in her uniform. She's got an old skirt that she bought at a vintage clothes shop. It's like something they used to wear in the sixties. It's quite heavy material and it's pleated all the way around in big, fat pleats, and it comes well below her knees. Also, she wears a long-sleeved white shirt that doesn't have a collar. She calls it a grandad shirt, but she always wears a baggy sweater over it. Her sweater is made of really soft, fine wool. Not like the regulation acrylic sweaters we're supposed to wear. She never seems to get hot. She wears thick, woolly tights. These are stripy, though you have to get quite close to see this because they're gray and black. Imogen wears black Doc Martens in the winter and black-and-white Converse sneakers in the summer. I think she looks dead cool and the teachers never complain that she's not in regulation uniform. Actually, I think some of the teachers are a bit in awe of her because I bet she's cleverer than some of them.

We've been best friends since primary school. Most girls seem to go around in groups of three or four, but Imogen and I just stick together. When we moved up to this school, some girls did try and attach themselves to us, but Imogen always seemed to put them off and if she's happy with it just being us two then so am I. Luckily for me she is never off sick and so far it's worked out all right.

I plonk myself down in the chair next to her. I want to tell her about the bus, and Sasha's remark, but I don't because I'm too embarrassed to repeat it, and, anyway, I know Imogen won't understand how awful it was because she never gets embarrassed about anything. She'd probably tell me that I should have told Sasha in a very loud voice that it's better to be a virgin than a skank. She doesn't understand that I could never, in a million years, do that. I can't not tell her about the new Sixth Former, though.

"There's a new boy in the Sixth Form," I say as casually as possible. "He's dead nice." I want to add, "and he actually spoke to me," but this doesn't sound very cool so I don't bother. Sometimes I wish Imogen wasn't so together and mature so we could have a good gossip about the new hunk and get all girly over him. I don't tell her that I know his name, because I want to keep it to myself.

I keep saying it in my head: Seth, Seth. It sounds like a sigh and I imagine myself whispering it, in a moment of passion, into his perfectly formed ear. I'm just about to drift off into a new daydream featuring myself and Seth when there's a commotion in the classroom. I look up and naturally Sasha is starring in the main role.

"You've all *got* to come. It's going to be the best party ever. But you can only get in with an invitation." She's handing these invitations out. She pauses by me and Imogen. "I don't want any crashers." And then she moves on.

Imogen has got her book out again and is reading.

"Did you see that?" I say, although I know she did.

"What?" Imogen doesn't even look up from her book.

"Sasha's given party invitations to everyone except us. She's even given one to Isobel Murray!" Sasha dislikes Isobel nearly as much as me, but obviously not quite as much. Sasha keeps glancing over at us. I turn my back on her and I can feel tears forming in my eyes and I hate myself for it. Imogen looks up and sees my face. She sighs.

"Would you go to her party if she'd given you an invitation?" she says to me.

"No way."

"Well, then, what's the problem?"

"I hate her."

"You shouldn't let her get to you. She's not worth it."

We've discussed this a thousand times. Imogen says that it's really her that Sasha doesn't like, but that Sasha knows Imogen doesn't care what she thinks so she picks on me instead because I always react to it. I know this is true and I've tried really hard to pretend I don't care, but even if I ignore her, I always give myself away by blushing.

Imogen is putting her book away. "It's quite funny, really," she says. "In order to make her point, Sasha has had to invite everyone except you and me—even the people she despises. So if they actually all turn up to her party she'll be really fed up."

She's got a point, and I smile at the thought of Sasha having to entertain all the greasy-haired geeks at her oh-so-cool party. She's obviously hoping that they won't go. By the time Mrs. Draycott comes in to take attendance, I'm feeling a lot better.

The first lesson is double art so the whole class traipses off to the art room. Usually I enjoy art, although I'm not particularly good at it. Art is Imogen's favorite subject and she is brilliant at drawing, but then her mum is an artist, so she's at an advantage there. When we arrive, Mrs. Burton isn't there so Sasha starts going on about her party in a loud voice, trying to wind me up.

I wander over to the still life, which we've been working on for the last few weeks. We're supposed to be doing it in different styles and, at the moment, I'm trying to do it in a cubist style and it's not working very well. The still life has been set up on a board in the corner and is beginning to look a bit sad. The apples are a tad wrinkly and the shiny teapot is beginning to lose its shine. I'm about to pick the whole thing up and carry it to the table in the middle when Sasha shouts out.

"Hey, look, everybody." She's over by Mrs. Burton's desk, waving a piece of paper. "It looks like Burty isn't coming in today. She's left this for the substitute. It says we're to get on with what we've been doing." She fakes an enormous yawn, screws the paper up into a ball, and throws it into the trash. Oh, great. That means that for the next two hours, Sasha is planning on winding up the class substitute and nobody will get any work done. Already Sasha's behavior has got everyone excited and the class is really rowdy now.

Beside me, Imogen sighs.

The door opens and the substitute walks in. Everybody sees her, but we all pretend that we haven't. She's not like the usual subs. For a start, she's a lot older and very efficient-looking. She looks more like a headmistress than our own headmistress. "My name is Miss Shears," she bellows.

Even a half blind two-year-old could tell that this is not a woman to mess with, but then Sasha doesn't seem to have as much intelligence as a two-year-old because she's still giggling away in the corner with her friends.

"Right. Enough. Silence!" Miss Shears's voice gets gradually louder with each word. "Why aren't you getting on with your work?"

Now we're all madly getting out our drawing boards and

paper, except Sasha, of course. She's tipping her chair back and filing her nails. "Mrs. Burton didn't leave us any," she says with a smirk.

Miss Shears's eyes narrow and she glances toward the waste basket. I just know that she's going to find the instructions and that Sasha will never own up to throwing them away and that the whole class will be in detention.

But I'm wrong; instead she strides over to where Sasha is sitting and puts her patent-leather shoe on the chair strut, bringing the chair down with a jolt. Even this doesn't knock any sense into Sasha, although she does look as though she's about to complain, and then thinks better of it. After all, Miss Shears hasn't actually touched her, thank God, or we would never hear the end of it.

"Right, I shall just have to think of something for you to do, then." She picks up a spare chair and places it on the desk in the middle of the room where I was going to put the still life. "I'd like you all to draw this."

Everybody groans, even Imogen, and some people glare accusingly at Sasha. Art is usually fun. Mrs. Burton believes in us expressing ourselves and there's no such thing as "going wrong." If you knocked a jar of paint over your work by accident, she'd just smile and say, "Incorporate it into the design."

This chair thing is a nightmare. It's torture. I glance over at Imogen, but she's got her tongue poking out a bit, a sure sign that she's concentrating, so I make an effort and start drawing, though I'm not really sure where to start. Do I start at the bottom and work upward or at the top and go down? What if I get to the bottom (or top) and find I've run out of paper and can't fit the thing on? I can feel a headache coming on. Eventually I decide to start in the middle with the seat bit, but the whole thing is so boring that I go off into a daydream.

It's not a full-blown daydream yet, I'm still evolving it. It involves me being so brilliant at art that the headmistress decides that I can do extra lessons after school. If you're thinking that's not much of a daydream, just wait. She decides that I need to do some life drawing, from a real-life nude, and when I turn up, there is Seth sitting on the chair—with nothing on. I'm concentrating really hard on imagining this when Miss Shears comes up behind me and says, "It could be a bit bigger, don't you think?" It takes me a moment to realize that she's talking about my drawing.

Having been around and looked at everyone's work, Miss Shears hands out more paper and says, "Right, I want you all to start again, only this time stop thinking of it as a chair. Start looking at it as a series of shapes. Don't draw the legs; draw the space between the legs." She goes up to the chair and pokes all the airy spaces with her finger. "Does anyone know what these are?"

Of course, nobody does. They're just nothing; I mean, how can you draw air?

"These," she says, "are negative shapes. Don't ignore them. They are just as important as these." Now she's poking the metal legs. "If it was a solid object, what shape would it be?"

Now I'm deeply confused but Imogen's hand shoots up. "A rectangle." She looks strangely happy.

"Exactly," says Miss Shears. She's drawing a three-dimensional oblong on the board and then she fits the chair into it. I see what she means now and my second attempt comes out much better, even if I say so myself. By the end of the lesson, everyone has a pretty good drawing, except Sasha and a few of her friends, who were just messing about most of the time and passing each other notes.

When the bell rings, we go off to math. Imogen is in the top group so I don't have this class with her and I traipse off with the middle group. Thankfully, Sasha is in the bottom group for math so I don't have to put up with her. I'm hopeless at math, but I work really hard at it, mainly so that I don't get put in the bottom group with her.

I sit down next to Lauren Hall. We usually sit together in math and while she's quite nice, she is very shy and it's not that easy talking to her. But today she seems to be making an effort, because she asks me if I'm going to Sasha's party.

"No," I tell her, "I haven't been invited."

"Oh, I don't think it matters," she says, "everybody's going."

I'm just wondering whether or not it's worth explaining to her that I have actually *not* been invited, rather than just overlooked, when Mr. Green comes in and we have to stop talking and get on with the lesson.

Chapter Five

At lunchtime I meet up with Imogen by the lockers. We're supposed to go outside at lunchtime and "get some fresh air." Just to make sure we do, they have Sixth Formers patrolling the school to throw us out. This is mean on so many levels. Firstly, we're too old to run around like the Year Seven and Eight kids, so we just stand around freezing to death. It's not so bad for the boys; at least they can play soccer. Also, it's not fair on the Sixth Formers. They get a nice common room to hang out in at lunchtimes and they hate it when they have to patrol the school, so they take it out on us if they find anyone inside. Today Imogen says, "Come on, let's go to the art room. If Burty's not here today she won't be hanging around."

"We'll only get chucked out by some grumpy Sixth Formers," I tell her.

"If any do come in we'll just tell them that we're tidying up for Burty. They can't check with her because she's not here." This seems like a good plan and beats freezing our tits off outside. I'd hate to lose what I've managed to grow so far, which isn't much, unlike Imogen who's been blessed in that department.

The art room isn't the best place in the world to eat lunch. It's filthy. Every surface is covered in dried-up paint, and the sink in the corner is a work of art in its own right. I reckon if Burty pulled it out and entered it in the next Turner Prize she'd stand a pretty good chance of winning.

Imogen starts drawing in her sketchbook and eating her lunch at the same time. I feel restless, though, and wander around the room eating my lunch as I go. Imogen is going on about the art lesson and how brilliant it was to actually be *taught* some drawing. Most of the time Imogen is sort of distant and self-contained but when she's excited about something, she gets really intense and won't stop talking. Sometimes the intense Imogen makes me uncomfortable. Maybe, deep down, I'm just shallow.

"I don't get it," I say to her. "You can draw really well already. And besides, can't your mum teach you? She's an artist."

Imogen's mum is so cool. Whenever I go around to their house she's in her studio, which is really the dining room, but she's taken it over. There's always a strong smell of turpentine and linseed oil, which can be a bit weird because it's next to the kitchen, and when it mingles with cooking smells the whole thing's a bit overpowering. She always has the radio on really loud, playing something classical and dramatic and really noisy. Because she gets so wrapped up in her work, housework doesn't come very high on Imogen's mum's list of priorities, and while I wouldn't go so far as to say their house is a dump, like ours, it is definitely chaotic, but in a good sort of artistic way, so that I always feel relaxed there. I often think that if I can't live with Dad then I'd like to live in Imogen's house. It's the sort of place where you could just be yourself and not get hassled all the time.

Imogen doesn't answer my question, and when I look over, she's got her tongue poking out so I know she's concentrating and probably didn't hear me. I think I'm restless because I'm thinking about Seth and I'd really like to talk about him, just so I can say his name. I think I must be going mad—I only met him this morning and I can't think about anything else anymore. Is this what love feels like? How can I love him? I don't even know him and I'm hardly likely to either. He's not going to be interested in a plain, nervous girl in Year Ten, for God's sake. What I need is to get a grip.

I'm over by the window, staring out, and I realize I'm scanning the playground for any sign of him. I can see a load of people hanging out down there, but of course there aren't any Sixth

Formers because they're all nice and cozy in their common room. The girls in my year who don't hang out with Sasha are all fooling around with each other and some of the boys from our year as well. I wonder what it would be like to be part of a big group like that and have friends that are boys and not "boyfriends." They look as though they're having fun. What would happen if I went and joined them? I know what would happen. It would be really awkward. They wouldn't actually be horrible to me, I don't think, but they'd wonder what the hell I was doing there and it would take ages to be accepted by them because I don't share their history. I wouldn't get all the inside jokes and stuff. Also, if I did any of that, Imogen would never talk to me again.

I'm just going off into a daydream in which Imogen is in a car crash or is really ill or something and doesn't come to school for ages (nothing too bad, of course, I'm not a complete monster) and everyone feels really sorry for me. I get accepted into their group and then when Imogen comes back she joins in as well, when we hear footsteps in the corridor outside the art room. Remembering what Imogen said about us pretending to tidy up, I start shuffling some pieces of paper around, trying to look busy. I'm expecting some Sixth Former to open the door and, for a minute, I imagine Seth coming in and my heart starts beating madly and I'm sure my face has gone red. So when the door does open and Luke O'Connor comes in, I'm not exactly behaving normally.

He walks over to me, but he's glancing nervously at Imogen all the time.

"Hi," he says.

"Hi," I say back. Now what? He's not looking at me, his eyes are focused somewhere over my shoulder, and I resist the urge to turn around and see what it is behind me that is so interesting. I've got a feeling that I know what's coming next and I go all hot and just know that I'm blushing again.

"I . . . um . . . I was wondering if you wanted to come to Sasha's party with me."

"I . . . I . . ." The power of speech seems to have left me. I'm spluttering. He looks horribly embarrassed and I desperately want to explain that I can't go because Sasha has made it plain that I'm *not* invited and that it's got nothing to do with me not wanting to go with him.

"She can't go," says Imogen from her seat in the middle of the classroom. "We are otherwise engaged."

Luke looks to me to confirm this and I try to smile and get the feeling that I'm grimacing instead, like I'm constipated or something.

"Okay. Sorry," he mumbles, and scoots from the room like it's suddenly on fire.

My heart is working overtime and I put my hand on my chest and will it to slow down. I can't believe someone's just asked me out. Okay, so it wasn't exactly the most romantic event of the year, but it was an event, for me at any rate. I've never been asked out before. If I'm feeling this churned up about it, imagine what Luke must be feeling? It must be really scary asking someone out. I'm sure if I was a boy I'd never have the nerve.

God! Why does everything have to be so difficult? Why couldn't I just explain to him? I feel really bad now. He'll think I don't like him. Why did Imogen have to stick her oar in? It's like she's my mother, telling him I can't come out to play. I realize I'm standing there with my mouth open as if I'm still waiting for some words to come out, and staring at Imogen.

She looks up. "What?" she says.

"Why did you have to say that to him?" I'm shouting at her—I can't believe I'm shouting at her—I've never shouted at Imogen before. What if she stops talking to me? I just want to explain that she's ruined a significant moment in my life.

"What do you mean? You weren't exactly saying anything . . . unless of course you want to turn up at Sasha's birthday party and be totally humiliated when she throws you out."

"No! I know . . . but that's not the point. I just . . ." I can't explain to her, because I don't know myself what the problem is. I know she's right and I should be grateful to her for coming to my rescue, because I wasn't exactly doing a good job myself. And even though I know all this I'm still cross with her. I'm cross that she barged in on my moment like that.

Imogen sighs. I've just noticed that she sighs a lot. It's beginning to get on my nerves.

"Anyhow," she says, "do you actually want to go out with Luke?"

Again, she has a point. Do I? I hadn't really considered this, to be honest. I was so amazed that someone had asked me out that I would probably have gone without thinking it through. At least I would have—if it hadn't been Sasha's party he was asking me to. I mean, it's not like it was William Gardner or Matt Weatherall who had asked me. Obviously then I would have said no immediately because they're both hopeless geeks. Not that they would ever ask any girl out—*because* they're hopeless geeks. Then again it's not like it was Spike Powell either. Then I would have said no because he's too dangerous. He's one of those people who are always getting into trouble, and he fancies himself as a ladies' man, when really he's just a thug. Not that Spike Powell would ask a girl like me out in a million years.

Luke O'Connor on the other hand isn't too bad. If I had to choose someone to ask me out I could do worse. In fact, thinking about it, I quite like him. Or do I? Maybe I just think I do because he asked me out. I can't say I've ever given him much thought up till now. . . . Aaarrgh. I think I'm going mad. From the look on Imogen's face she clearly thinks so, too.

An imaginary date with Luke flashes through my head. We meet up in town and go for a coffee. It's a bit strained at first—between us I mean, not the coffee. I don't know what we'd talk about so I imagine that some friends come in and join us. It's obviously imaginary, because these girls wouldn't normally have coffee with me, but hey! Who cares? Also, bizarrely, Lauren Hall is being all chatty and entertaining and she sweeps through the door of the café and goes, "Alice! How lovely to see you," making Luke think that I'm popular and sought after.

Then the girls disappear, because this is a date after all, and we're in the park, just hanging out on the swings and stuff and then we're walking and he takes my hand and he holds it all the way to the cinema where we see a romantic comedy together. We're sitting in the back row and there's hardly anyone else in there, and he leans over to kiss me and everything's all right because I've just eaten a packet of mints so I'm not worried about having dog breath or anything, and our lips meet. . . . It gets a bit hazy here because I've never actually had a proper kiss with a boy and I don't know if I'm supposed to hold my breath—I mean how do you breathe when you've got your mouth clamped to somebody else's—and do you keep your mouth closed or should it be open? But never mind all that now, we're kissing and I have my eyes closed, and when we stop and I open them it isn't Luke sitting next to me in the cinema—it's Seth.

Imogen is still staring at me as if I'm mad, though now she's starting to look a bit concerned. I snap out of my daydream and try to appear normal and together.

"I'm sorry," she says. "Did you want to go out with Luke?"

"No, not really." I flop down into the chair next to her. "But you should have let me deal with it."

"Okay, next time I'll leave it to you, but I should point out that most people communicate using words—so you might want to think of some in case it happens again."

I feel like someone's scrambled my brain in a food processor. And all my insides, as well. I feel emotionally drained. I'd quite like to go home and curl up in bed and shut the world out, but I can't because it's French next and then Tech Ed so I'll just have to pull myself together.

Imogen looks at her watch and starts packing her things away. I wonder if she realizes how close we came to having an argument. We've never argued before, certainly never fallen out. I feel a bit ashamed at how cross with her I was. I should have known that nothing gets past Imogen, though, because she says, "Look, let's promise that a boy will never come between us," and suddenly everything is all right again.

When it's time to go home, Imogen waits at the bus stop with me. She lives in the opposite direction and usually disappears as soon as the bell goes, but today she hangs around. I try not to make it too obvious that I'm keeping an eye out for Seth and try to concentrate on what she's saying.

". . . so I thought that as everybody in the entire world will be at Sasha's party on Saturday night, why don't you come over to my place and we can have our own party. Or at least we could get a DVD out and have a night in. What do you think?"

"Hmm?" I've just spotted Seth coming toward the bus stop with a couple of his friends.

"Alice, are you listening to me?"

"What?"

"Houston to planet Alice . . . are you receiving me? Come in, come in."

I tear my eyes away from the gorgeousness that is Seth and, remembering our pact earlier in the art room, I focus on Imogen.

"That'll be great," I say, and I mean it, too. I love going to Imogen's and I wish I went more often, but it's difficult with her living two bus journeys away. Then, over her shoulder, I spot Seth coming toward me. He's looking at me and smiling—he's definitely coming over to talk to me! I desperately don't want to talk to him while Imogen's there so I say, "I'll call you," and dash off in his direction. I daren't look back to see if Imogen is watching.

"Hi, thank goodness! A friendly face at last," Seth says to me. My heart is in my mouth, but I manage to smile without it falling out at his feet.

"We're just going into town for a coffee, do you fancy it?"

Oh, my God! I can't believe this is happening. I don't know who the "we" is, but I don't really care. I can't pass up a chance like this.

"Sure, why not?" I say all casually.

Then I remember that I've got to pick up Rory from Mrs. Archer's. Damn! As we're walking into town, I call Mrs. Archer and tell her that I might be a bit late. She's completely unfazed by this and tells me it's no problem, she'll just hang on to him until I get there.

"I hope I'm not keeping you from anything important," says Seth when I've hung up. Is he crazy? What could be more important than him? Obviously I don't tell him that, at least not this early in the relationship.

I'm trying to work out how I can take a sneaky picture of him with my camera phone so that I can drool over it later when I'm alone in my room. I decide not to risk it because it would be *so* embarrassing if he realized what I was doing. I don't want him to think I'm too desperate and immature. Even though I am.

Calm down, I tell myself, and concentrate on my breathing for a bit until I notice Seth giving me a funny look and realize that I've been breathing out loud.

When we get to the coffee shop, I begin to panic a bit. Well, a lot actually. It's full of Sixth Formers and I'm positive they're all giving me funny looks, especially the girls. I'm beginning to wish I hadn't come. How could I have been so impulsive?

What on earth are we going to talk about? I consider rushing to the bathroom and escaping out of the window but Seth is asking me what sort of coffee I want and I don't know, so I say the first thing I see on the board, which is "Turkish Black." It sounds quite sophisticated and yummy, like Turkish Delight. Although everyone says "hi" to Seth as we pass them, he doesn't stop to chat to anyone. Instead he leads me to a table in the corner. I'm so relieved I could kiss him. Then I wish I hadn't thought that because it's made me blush.

While I'm madly trying to think of something to say, I take a sip of my coffee and nearly drop down dead. I've never tasted anything so repulsive. Well, not since the time Rory slipped Mum's Chanel No. 5 into my orange juice, that is. Then, I threw up for about two hours, nonstop, but that is not an option today. Not on a first date.

I'd love to pour some milk into the coffee to take the edge off it, but I've got a feeling it would take about six pints to stop it looking black, because it's so strong. And it's in a teeny-weeny cup, as well. What a rip-off. I'm so absorbed in the coffee issue that I forget to be nervous and before I know it, Seth and I are chatting away like we've known each other forever. It turns out that although he's always lived locally, he's been away at boarding school since he was eleven, but decided to come home for the Sixth Form because they didn't get enough freedom there, and besides it was a single-sex school and he was fed up with single sex. I go bright red at the mention of sex and laugh nervously— then shut up quickly in case I sound hysterical.

Then we both have a good moan about our families. Seth's parents are divorced as well, but his dad has just remarried and he's living with him and the new family most of the time because he doesn't get on with his mum's new boyfriend, although he says it's a bit of a toss up as to which is worse: his mum's boyfriend or his new stepsister. She sounds like the stepsister from hell. I tell him about "the little brother from hell" and how awful my mum is, but I don't tell him that I'm hoping to go and live with Dad because I don't want to jinx it. I'll wait until I've arranged it and then tell him. If he wants to see me again, that is.

Eventually, I tear my eyes away from Seth and look around the café. I want to see if the Sixth Form girls are noticing how well we're getting on. Pathetic, I know, but I've never been so happy. I realize that the rest of the people from school, who were here when we arrived, have all disappeared and been replaced by adults in suits who have obviously just finished work.

"Oh, my God! What time is it?" I ask Seth, panic creeping into my voice.

"Five-twenty. Is there a problem?"

God, I hope not. I'm struggling to get my blazer on when my phone rings. I grab it and fumble with the buttons. I don't recognize the number. It can't be Dad or Trish or even Mrs. Archer because my phone would recognize those numbers. I'm about to answer it when Seth says, "Can I see you on Saturday?" so I turn it off.

"Yes." I hope I haven't answered too quickly. It's difficult not to sound keen when you're so keen you could die.

"Here's my number," he says, pushing a napkin into my hand. "Call me."

"Thanks, got to go," and I grab my bag and run.

Chapter Six

Sitting on the bus, I grab my phone to see if I can work out who it was that rang me, and it rings again and I nearly drop it. This time it's a text. It says, *Where are you?* Oh, my God! It must be Seth, and we've only been parted about five minutes. I'm about to reply, *On Cloud Nine* when I remember that he doesn't have my number. I get out the napkin to check, and sure enough it isn't him. Great, my first phone call and I don't even know who it is. What if it's some perv randomly dialing numbers, hoping to get an unsuspecting girl to reply. I think about texting *Mind your own business*, but decide that if it is some perv I'd be better off ignoring it. I hope this phone isn't going to be more trouble than it's worth. Then I remember I've got Seth's number, and I'm back on Cloud Nine.

When I reach Mrs. Archer's front gate, I have to stop and get my breath back. I ring the bell and fix a smile on my face, all ready to apologize profusely. But when she answers the door she tells me that Mum picked Rory up half an hour ago.

Hell! Now I'm in for it. Mum will want to know where I've been, and I'll probably be grounded. She'll go on at me about how she's had to pay Mrs. Archer for an extra two hours and I'll scream back that she shouldn't treat me like an unpaid slave—that *she's* Rory's mother, not me, that I need a life. . . . Anyhow, when I go and live with Dad she'll realize how much she uses me and then she'll get a reality check.

Still, it's not going to be pretty, I think as I open the front door. Oh, God! What if she stops me from going to Imogen's on Saturday? Aaargh! Saturday! Seth! Imogen! I've double booked! I need to go and shut myself in my room so that I can think this through, but the minute I open the front door Mum's there giving me The

Look. Before I even think about it I'm saying, "Sorry, Mum—I had a detention." Wow, where did that come from?

"A detention? Why?"

"Oh, nothing drastic," I lie. "It wasn't even my fault. Someone passed me a note and I got the blame." Mum is not looking particularly convinced.

"I thought they had to give twenty-four hours' notice, and, anyway, why are you so late? I thought detentions only lasted an hour." How come my mum is suddenly an expert on detentions? I've never had one before. Even I didn't know all that.

"Yeah, I'm sorry, I forgot to mention it yesterday, and then I had to get off the bus a stop early so I could go to the drugstore and get some *things*," I say, looking meaningfully at Rory who has just joined us in the hall.

Finally Mum seems to have swallowed all these amazing lies that keep popping out of my mouth. "Well, you should have rung. I rang you and texted you, I was just starting to get worried." I follow her into the kitchen.

"What do you mean you texted me?" Then I spot a cell phone on the table.

"I got Gwen at work to teach me." Mum looks a bit sheepish. "The thing is, love, I bought this phone for you." She picks up the phone. "I was going to give it to you for your birthday but then Dad gave you one, and well . . . I thought I might as well keep it and then we can stay in touch when I'm not here. . . ."

Oh, great. My worst nightmare. She might as well have sewn the umbilical cord back on.

"How did you get my number?" I know I sound grumpy but I can't help it.

"I called your dad and he gave it to me. Like I say, I was worried."

I look at the phone in Mum's hand and suddenly realize why she got so upset when Dad gave me a phone. It wasn't because she didn't want me to have one and it wasn't even about the money. It was because she was planning on giving me one for my birthday.

She must have saved up for it for ages, even though it looks like quite a cheap one. I know I'm being horrid. This always happens when I feel bad. It's like, by being angry, I can cover up the fact that really I feel sad. I think about Mum looking forward to giving me the phone on my birthday and I feel like crying. Instead I shout, "Well, don't think you can call me every minute of the day."

Mum looks hurt, which makes me even more angry, so I shout even louder as I leave the room, "And don't expect me to look after Rory on Saturday, because I'm going to Imogen's for the night."

When I've shut myself in my room, I lie on my bed, exhausted. I've got a tight knot of anger in my chest, but at the same time I feel ecstatic because of Seth. I decide to concentrate on the ecstatic bit for the moment and drift off into a wild and wonderful daydream that encompasses all my former daydreams.

I'm living at Dad's, in the new house, with my supercool bedroom, and Trish and Dad have gone away on their honeymoon leaving me on my own for a whole week. Of course, Seth comes to stay to keep me company. We go out for long romantic walks in the park and by the canal, holding hands, and when we stop to look at the ducklings, he stands behind me and wraps his arms around me and I lean back into his hard, broad chest. Then it's snowing and we're in the park goofing around, throwing snow at each other and eventually we end up rolling around laughing and making snow angels, and then he's kissing me . . . mmm . . . and then we're at home and we're snuggled up on the sofa in front of the fire, watching a romantic film together and sharing pizza and popcorn and then we're kissing again and I realize that soon it will be time for bed. . . .

There's a banging on my bedroom door. Bloody Rory. "Mum says dinner's ready." He's rattling the door handle but I've wedged a chair under it so he can't get in. I roll off the bed.

"Go away. Tell her I don't want any."

He thuds down the stairs with the message. He loves carrying messages to and from Mum and me, which is just as well because that way I don't actually have to talk to her. The trouble is, I'm starving and I really do want my dinner, but I don't want to leave my room and have to face reality. Not after such an awesome daydream. I wonder where it would have gone if Rory hadn't interrupted it. I've never really kissed a boy before, let alone anything else. I don't really want to think about the "anything else." The kissing is good enough for now. The only trouble is, will it be good enough for Seth? I think back to the joke he made in the café about being fed up with single sex. Was he trying to tell me something?

I can hear Mum calling me and suddenly I don't want to be on my own anymore with all these thoughts, so I go downstairs.

I manage to get through the meal without being interrogated by pulling a mega-sulk. I leave as soon as possible, mumbling something about heaps of homework, and hurry back to my room. I get my phone out and put Seth's number into it, then carefully place the napkin that he wrote it on in my treasure box. I lock it then hide the key in the closet, in the pocket of an old jacket that I never wear anymore. You can never be too careful with a brother like Rory around.

When Seth said "call me," did he mean tonight? Would that seem a bit desperate if I called him now? Then again, when he said could we meet up on Saturday did he mean during the day or in the evening? If he meant the day then I won't have to worry because I can still go to Imogen's later. But if he meant the evening, then what am I going to do about Imogen? I could just call her and say I can't make it. But then she'll want to know why and I can't tell her about Seth because if she thinks I'm canceling on her because of a boy she'll never speak to me again. It's no good—I've got to find out from Seth when I'm going to see him. Maybe I'll just text him.

I go into messages and realize that this will be the first text I've ever sent. I type in *Hi* and sit for ages wondering what else to put. *Wot time Sat* would be a good idea, but in the end I just leave it as it is and send *Hi* all on its own. I'm just sitting there thinking that he won't know who it's from because I'm not in his phone index and maybe I should send a proper message, when my phone rings, nearly giving me a heart attack. *Seth* comes up on the screen and I think I must get a photo of him and then that will come up as well.

"Hi," I say into the phone.

Seth's voice comes back. "I thought it was you. Either that, or someone going for the world record in shortest text ever."

I decide to get straight to the point. "I was just wondering what time you wanted to meet up on Saturday."

"Well, I've got a Saturday job and that finishes at five so I thought about sevenish if that's okay with you? Shall I pick you up at your place?"

Hell, no. That won't do. I need a plan. Thinking quickly I say, "I'll get back to you on that. I'm not sure where I'm going to be." Well, that's the truth. We talk for a bit longer, then he says, "God, I can hear my stepsister coming. I'll have to go, see you on Saturday," and he's gone.

Later, in bed, I try to get back into my daydream—the one that had been so rudely interrupted earlier—but it's no good. I need to put my mind to how I'm going to see Imogen and Seth on Saturday night. Why couldn't I have just told Seth that I had plans and that we'd have to leave it till another time? Partly because I want to see him—desperately—and partly because I don't want him to think I'm not interested.

As it turns out, I have the whole night to hatch a plan because, thanks to that Turkish coffee, I don't get a wink of sleep. And on the whole it's not a bad plan. It could be better, but I think it will work.

Chapter Seven

I don't see Seth at all during the week. I spend every day in a state of nervous anticipation and don't even notice Sasha's snide remarks when I get on the bus every morning. I'm too busy scanning the back rows for a sight of him. By Friday, I'm beginning to wonder if I imagined the whole thing.

I spend the morning break hoping that he'll come and find me and fearful in case he does and I have to explain him to Imogen. I would have gone through the same agonies at lunchtime, no doubt, only I hear someone saying that most of the Sixth Formers are away on a trip or something. I'm hugely relieved because now I can stop worrying about bumping into him and also because I've finally heard someone talking about something other than Sasha's birthday party. It's certainly all Sasha's been talking about all week, raising her voice on the subject whenever Imogen and I are in the vicinity. It's driving me insane. What's more, next week we'll have to endure her going on about how awesome it was, who she spent the night snogging, how many cool Sixth Formers turned up, etc., etc., ad infinitum. Aaaarrgh!

Imogen and I decide to meet up in town on Saturday morning, do some shopping and then go back to her house. She wanted to meet up in the afternoon but I persuade her to make it earlier because I don't want to be stuck at home all morning with Mum and Rory. Saturday mornings are when Mum "tries to catch up on the housework" and attempts to rope me in, totally disregarding the fact that Saturday mornings are when I like to catch up on a bit of sleep.

The first time I met Imogen's mum she told me to call her Claire. "Mrs. Crawford sounds so stuffy, don't you think?" she said to me, like I was a grown-up and not a little girl of seven, which I was at the time.

Not that I get much chance to call her anything, mind you, because I don't go to Imogen's very often, and when I do, we spend most of our time in her bedroom so that we don't disturb Claire's "artistic flow." She seems to wander around in an artistic trance most of the time.

I wonder if Imogen knows how lucky she is to have such a laid-back mum. One who isn't always out at work and worrying about everything. Also, it must be great to have something in common. They're both totally into art. I can't think of one tiny thing that Mum and I have in common, except that we hate each other and I don't think that counts.

When I meet up with Imogen on Saturday, she tells me that she has to go to the art shop because she needs to buy some felt pens.

"Can't you get them at WHSmith's?" I say, because the art shop is such a long walk.

"No, they're special ones," she informs me quite sharply. She's in a mood today so I decide not to complain too much and we set off a bit too briskly for my liking. It's all right for her. She's not carrying a bag, but I'm lugging all my overnight things with me. Which is really annoying, because if my plan works then I won't actually need any of them. As I hurry along beside Imogen, I go over the plan in my head to check that I've got it straight. When I left the house this morning, I told Mum I was going to spend the night at Imogen's and I packed all my stuff—except I made sure I had a stunning outfit in the bag. Well, I say stunning, I don't actually own anything *stunning*, unless of course Seth is stunned by how lame I look. I have a bit of a problem with clothes, to tell the truth. Everything I own is deadly boring and I can't even raid Mum's wardrobe because everything in there is even more boring than my stuff, if that is at all possible.

So sometime in the afternoon when I'm at Imogen's, I'll change for my date with Seth, and then at about half past six, I'll tell Imogen that I've had a call from Mum asking me to go home because she has to go into work—some emergency or other—and needs me to look after Rory. I'll then leave Imogen's and go and meet Seth. Then, depending what time the date finishes, I'll either go back to Imogen's and tell her the emergency is over and Mum came home, or if it's too late I'll have to go home and tell Mum that there was an emergency at Imogen's—a sick aunt or something, and they all had to leave suddenly. It's not as complicated as it seems, honestly.

It just boils down to Imogen thinking I've gone home and Mum thinking that I'm at Imogen's, and all the time I'm out with Seth. It's just the last bit that's slightly up in the air, but by that time I'll have had a brilliant time with the most gorgeous boy in the world and I'm sure it will all fall into place.

By the time I've run through this plan for the hundredth time, we arrive at the art shop. Unfortunately, it's not a case of going in, finding the pens, paying for them, and leaving. When we get in there, the shop owner seems to know Imogen and starts asking after her mum, saying what a good customer she is. Eventually we manage to escape and make our way down the aisles of tightly packed shelves until we get to the "special" felt pens, though I don't know what's special about them.

Then it takes ages to work out if it would be cheaper to buy them individually or in a pack, which has 20 percent off, and are the ones in the pack the right color, etc., etc., until I feel like screaming. Eventually she decides on a pack and a couple of loose ones. When we get to the cash register, I nearly faint at the price but the man tells her she can have a discount, "on account of her mum." Imogen looks like she wants the floor to open up and swallow her. She can't get out of there fast enough, but when we do finally reach the pavement, she won't tell me what the problem is.

I'm a bit miffed by now because, apart from the fact that we've now got to walk all the way back into town, it's too late to do any serious shopping. I was hoping to find a new bra, you know, one of those push-up ones that make you look like you've got more than you really have. I certainly need all the help I can get in that department. I was also hoping to find something really great that I can wear tonight. The outfit in my bag isn't exactly ideal for a night out with the coolest boy on the planet. I feel really on edge, sort of excited and terrified at the same time. I've never been on a date before and I don't know what to expect. Most of all I don't want to make a fool of myself or look too young or blush too often. I *so* wish I could talk it over with Imogen, or anyone for that matter.

I remember my gran used to cook things in a pressure cooker. It was a huge great saucepan with a tightly sealed lid and all this steam built up inside it until eventually it came hissing out the top. I was terrified of the thing and refused to go in the kitchen when she was using it because I was convinced it was going to blow up and cover everyone and everything with hot stew. Well, that's what I feel like: a pressure cooker. Actually, that thought has made me really miss my gran. If she was still alive, I could talk to her about everything. I can feel tears welling up behind my eyes. Why does life have to be so complicated? If I wasn't seeing Seth tonight I would be more relaxed and could be having fun with Imogen. Mind you, she's marching along with a face sullen enough to scare the spots off a dalmatian. I don't know what's up with her. Perhaps I should ask her.

"What's up?" I say, trying to keep up. You'd think she was embarrassed by me the way she's walking three steps ahead all the time. She stops suddenly so I bump into her and glares at me, like it's my fault.

"What do you mean, 'What's up'?"

Whoa, tread carefully. What I don't need right now is an argument. "Well, you know . . . I just thought you looked a bit—"

"What?" she snaps back. "A bit what?"

"Oh, you know . . ." I flounder. "Maybe a tad . . . distracted," I finish, madly trying to avoid the words sulky, sullen, surly, miserable, morose, moody, and downright dismal.

"Yeah, well . . . you know . . . it's just that . . . the thing is . . ."

It's so unlike Imogen to falter where words are concerned. That's usually my job.

"Look . . . when we get back to my place . . ."

I nod in what I hope is an encouraging way.

"Just try and avoid my mum as much as possible."

God! Is that all?! I can relate to that one. Maybe falling out with her mum is a new one for Imogen. I, on the other hand, am experienced beyond my years in such matters. I'm mightily relieved that I can help her with this.

"No problem," I tell her. "I'm well qualified in Mum Avoidance."

"It's just that my dad had to go away for a couple of days on business and Mum gets a bit . . . she just gets . . . she misses him . . . gets a bit stressed."

I bite my tongue. Gone away for two days? You want to try seven years, I think, and then see how stressed things will get!

"Thank God he's coming back tonight." Imogen suddenly looks more cheerful. We're back in town now and she manages a smile and asks me what I want to do.

"Okay," I say, looking down at my trainers, jeans, and totally nondescript top. "What I want is to look less like a little girl and more . . . well, you know . . . more . . . just older."

I think Imogen is going to laugh at me, but she doesn't. Instead she looks me up and down, stands back a bit and scrutinizes me with her head on one side and says, "Hmm, I see what you mean." I'm not at all offended, just relieved. "How much money have you got?" she asks, all business-like. If there's one thing Imogen loves, it's organizing people.

"Not much," I tell her. I emptied out my piggy bank this morning and I've got about thirty pounds on me, but I might need some tonight so I can't spend it all.

"Right," she says, looking at her watch, "let's hit the thrift shops."

"Are you mad?" I squawk. "When I said I wanted to look older, I meant about seventeen, not seventy!"

"Don't panic," she says. "When did you last go in a thrift shop? It's not all baggy skirts and camel-hair coats, you know. You can pick up some really decent stuff if you look carefully. Some thrift shops only take designer labels now. Come *on*!" she says, literally dragging me into the Oxfam shop. "Just think of it as recycling," she adds, rifling through the racks. At first, I'm deadly embarrassed, but after awhile I begin to wonder why. The shop is full of all sorts of people, young and old, trendy and square. We have a laugh at some of the stuff on the rails, things that even my mum wouldn't be seen dead in. But she's right, there are some okay things and I find a really nice pair of low-rise black jeans, which look miles better than the blue ones I've got on, and in Cancer Research I find a dead cool Joe Bloggs tie-dyed top. I can't believe it. And I haven't had so much fun in ages. Even Imogen seems to be enjoying herself, and we spend ages in Superdrug testing all the cosmetics, then I drag her into Boots and sniff all the perfumes until I find one I like and spray it all over my neck. Seth won't be able to resist me!

Chapter Eight

We're still in high spirits when we get back to Imogen's house and I can't wait to get into my new clothes and try out the lip gloss I bought. It takes me awhile to realize Imogen's brooding mood has returned. She silently indicates to me to put my bag down at the bottom of the stairs, then practically creeps down the hall to the kitchen. Not that we need to creep. There's some very loud classical music coming from the back of the house where Imogen's mum has her painting studio. The music gets louder as we enter the kitchen and now Imogen is using sign language, not because she wants to go undetected but because I wouldn't be able to hear her if she did say anything. Imogen looks at me apologetically and shrugs her shoulders. Wordlessly, she goes to the fridge and passes me some milk and a chunk of Edam cheese.

I look around the kitchen. It seems to be more chaotic than usual. Actually, *chaotic* is a polite term for revoltingly messy. The sink is full of dirty dishes and on closer inspection it's not just crockery in there. The cups and plates are jumbled together with painting paraphernalia, causing a tide mark of greasy black paint. Old food smells are mingling with the strong smell of turpentine and linseed oil. I know it's linseed oil because there's a big bottle of it that's fallen over on the drainboard, the thick oil snaking its way to a puddle in the sink around the dishpan. If the music wasn't so loud I'd suggest perhaps we should tidy the place up a bit, but Imogen is looking like a thundercloud and would probably take it the wrong way.

She's found some cream crackers and chocolate cookies in the cupboard and is indicating with her eyes toward the kitchen door, which I take to mean, "Let's get the hell out of here." As I try to exit, clutching the milk and the Edam, I run slap bang into Imogen's dad, whom we didn't hear come home on account of the music. I manage to stop the milk from ending up all over the floor at the expense of the cheese, which falls with a thud at her dad's feet. (I think he's called Clive, but I'm not sure, so hope I never have to address him directly.) We're all standing there staring at each other when suddenly the music stops abruptly, as if some sixth sense has alerted Claire to the arrival of Clive, and the double doors that separate the kitchen from what should be a dining room, but is now Claire's studio, are flung open with a flourish.

"Darling!" cries Claire, rushing past Imogen, who nearly ends up with her bottom in the trash can as she steps back out of the way. Claire is wearing an ankle-length black dress, some floaty scarf-type thing, and her hair is swept up in an intricate design. It's only as she passes me that I see it's held up with a paint brush, and not a clean one at that. She looks as though she's about to go out to a very posh party, except that she's covered from head to foot in splotches of paint.

"God! She's a bloody walking cliché," Imogen mutters, and although I'm not exactly sure what she means, I get the impression it's not good.

Claire falls into Clive's arms. They start kissing in a way that can only be described as *passionate*. Bloody hell! I'm tempted to watch so I can get some tips for later, but frankly it's embarrassing. I sneak a look at Imogen to see if she's embarrassed, too, but she just looks bored. Not knowing where else to look I find myself staring into the studio. There's an enormous canvas in there, but it appears to be painted completely black. Maybe it's an undercoat or something. Imogen grabs me and we sidle around the reunion going on in the doorway. I think about retrieving the cheese but Claire's three-inch heel is now impaling it to the floor.

"Hi, Dad," Imogen says as we pass, and he replies with something that I imagine is probably "Hi there, darling," but he's having trouble as Claire seems to have her tongue firmly down his throat. Yeeurk! Gross, I mean they must be in their forties!

As we go up the stairs, I surreptitiously look at my watch. After all, I have a schedule to keep to. It's quarter to three, which means I've got just over two hours to make myself look beautiful before I have to put stage one of my plan into action.

Imogen's bedroom is amazing. For starters, it's massive and has different "areas." There's her working area, which has a massive desk, except it's not like one you'd buy in a shop—it goes across one whole wall. It's been custom built to fit everything, so it's got a writing bit at one end, a computer in the middle, and a space for artwork at the end. I wonder if I'd be as clever and creative as Imogen if I had such a desk. I notice that at one end of it she's got a kettle and one of those minifridges. In fact, it's more like a studio apartment than a bedroom. I am so jealous. If I had a room like this I'd never have to leave it or see Mum and Rory at all. Halfway along the other wall is a television, which can be turned so it can be seen from the sitting area in the big bay window where the sofa is or from the big bed, which is practically a double.

Imogen has put the kettle on and gets her new felt pens out of her bag. Stuck on the wall above her art area are loads of pictures that she's drawn. I go over and have a look. They're incredible. They're like cartoons, only I can tell straight away who they are.

"Manga," says Imogen. "That's what I needed the pens for."

The biggest drawing is clearly a picture of Sasha. Imogen has made her look really evil. I realize they're like the drawings on a program that Rory watches called *Yu-Gi-Oh*. They look really professional. "They're . . . brilliant," I tell her. I really want to ask her if she'll do one of Seth for me. But I can't. Not yet, anyway.

"Look," says Imogen, going over to the computer. She hits a button and the screensaver disappears. I notice that she's going on the Internet and wonder if she has unrestricted access. And if she knows how lucky she is. A site comes up with the heading *Bishop Aubrey College*.

"This is where I'm going in September," she says. "It's a

boarding school and it's brilliant. I can't wait! I don't know why I didn't think of it before. Look at all the stuff they do there." She's scrolling down the page and I'm trying to take in the pictures of the grounds and the bedrooms and the tennis courts and the swimming pool. They've even got their own theater. She pauses on the art block.

"This is the best bit," she says, pointing at the screen. There's a photo of a big airy studio. It's been partitioned off into cubicles. "See! I'll get my own space to do my drawing in. They even have life models to draw from."

I stare at her openmouthed. "What! You mean you won't be going back to school after the summer? You can't . . . Do you mean you're leaving? You can't," I finish feebly.

"Look," she says, pointing to the website. "It's amazing. People from all over the world go there. Dad's already agreed. I seriously can't wait. And look at this," she says, scrolling on to pictures of some very gorgeous-looking people on skiing trips, another taken outside the Colosseum in Rome, and another showing some sweaty teenagers trekking through what looks like a very dense jungle. "The best thing is that I don't even have to come home in the holidays. A lot of the students there have parents who work abroad and stuff, so they have this holiday club."

I can't believe it. How could she do this to me? I want to cry. I want to shout at her that she can't go and leave me alone in my boring life. But most of all I want to go to this amazing school. She looks so bloody happy I could strangle her.

"But it's so"—I desperately want to put her off the idea— "so far outside your comfort zone." I can't think of anything else to say.

Imogen turns and stares at me. I blush, thinking that I had just sounded a bit like some TV psychologist.

"I don't have a 'comfort zone,'" she says. She's hunched over her keyboard tapping away at something, and it occurs to me that even though Imogen is my best friend I don't really know much about her. Like what she does when we're not at school, what sort of a relationship she has with her parents—things like that.

"Look at this," she says, nodding toward the computer. She's left the school website and, as far as I can tell, is now on some sort of chat website. I lean in closer, wondering what she's up to.

She's posting a message up.

Come to the best party of the year! Loud music, free booze, all the food you can eat, and girls, girls, girls!!!!

Underneath is an address.

"What is it?" I ask.

"An invitation to the world—to Sasha's party. I thought it would be a laugh—and serve her right for being such a cow."

I have a very bad feeling about this, but I keep my thoughts to myself. I'm still trying to come to terms with the fact that Imogen is abandoning me. I don't want to argue with her, though. I need her on my side if I'm going to carry out my plan. I decide to cash in on her good humor before it evaporates again.

"Come on," I say, "don't forget you promised to help me look older."

"Oh, hell," says Imogen, looking me up and down. "Where to start?"

"Thanks!"

"I'm only kidding." She laughs. "I'll have you looking amazing in no time."

This, I soon discover, is a bit of an exaggeration, as it takes Imogen a good two hours of hard work until I look anywhere near acceptable. While I'm in the shower washing my hair, Imogen rinses out the top I bought because it smells a bit musty, and sticks it in the dryer. Then she does my hair. She rubs some mousse stuff into it and puts it in huge curlers, which she's stole from her mum's room. I feel like a complete idiot but Imogen insists it will be worth it. Then she helps me with my makeup. This is the tricky part because I don't want to look as though I'm wearing any. But I needn't worry because Imogen is an artist after all, and she's got loads of makeup for someone who appears not to be too bothered about how she looks. She uses brown mascara, some very subtle eyeliner, a bit of powder, especially on my forehead where I've got an outcrop of zits, and my new lip gloss. When she takes the curlers out, my hair is wavy but nothing too obvious. I can't believe the transformation, and when I've got the new clothes on I feel great.

I'm *certain* these black jeans make me look slimmer. Some of my nerves have disappeared. Until, that is, I realize it's nearly six o'clock and I need to put my plan into action.

I get my phone out of my bag and I'm staring at it, trying to work out how I can convince Imogen that I've got a call from my mum. I'm just about to start fiddling with it to see if I can get into the ring tones and set one off—when it rings and I nearly have a heart attack. It's Mum.

"Alice, I'm really sorry to do this to you, but I need you to come home."

I can't believe it. There I am, about to pretend that my mum's calling to tell me I have to go home, and then she actually does!

"What! What do you mean? I can't come home! I'm at Imogen's for the night." The realization that I won't be able to see Seth kicks in. "I'm not coming home," I shout at her.

"Look, I wouldn't ask you unless it was really important, Alice. Please . . . only I've just had a call from work . . ."

That does it! Her and her bloody work! "Tell them you can't work tonight. It's the truth—you can't go to work because I'm not bloody well coming home." By the time I've finished, I'm shouting, and with a final screech I throw the phone onto the floor. I desperately want to cry, but I don't want my mascara to run. Not that it matters now. I hardly need to look nice for babysitting Rory.

Imogen picks the phone up and puts it to her ear.

"Hello, Susan. It's Imogen here . . . Oh . . . I see . . . I'm sorry . . . Okay . . . My dad can give her a lift. No, don't worry . . . it's no bother, we can do it another night."

I glare at Imogen. How dare she collude with my mother in this way, and why is she agreeing with her?

Imogen hangs up and passes me the phone. "She doesn't have to go to work," she says quietly. "It's Miss Maybrooke. Your mum's work phoned to say that Miss Maybrooke is really ill . . . dying actually . . . and she's asking for your mum."

I swallow. I feel really bad now. Imogen is obviously not impressed by my outburst. But how was I supposed to know?

"I'll go and ask Dad to run you home," she says. When she's gone I pack my bag and then pick up the phone. I suppose I'll have to text Seth now and tell him I can't make it. But then a plan starts to form in my head—a Plan B. I stuff the phone into my bag and when Imogen comes back and says her dad can take me home, I beg her to come with me.

"Go on, Imo . . . it'll be great. You can spend the night at my house instead . . ." She looks unconvinced. "Pleeease . . . it'll be better than having the whole night ruined. We can still watch the DVD. We can order pizza."

Imogen hesitates. I can see that she's thinking it won't be a bundle of laughs at my place, what with Miss Maybrooke and everything. But when she came back into the room she left the door open and the loud, dramatic, classical music is floating up the stairs. And then we hear her mother laugh, a high, almost hysterical sound, and that seems to do the trick.

"Okay, why not?" she says, and stuffs some things into a bag. I've never seen anyone get ready so quickly.

"Let's go," she says and is halfway down the stairs before I've even got to the bedroom door. Somehow I get the feeling that her haste has less to do with the fact that Miss Maybrooke might breathe her last before Mum gets there than the fact that she seems desperate to get out of her house.

Chapter Nine

On the way home in the car, I'm worried that Mum will ask me why I'm all dressed up, but I needn't have worried on that score. As soon as we get in, Mum hurriedly says hello to Imogen and me and then hurriedly says good-bye and disappears out the door.

I look at my watch. It's quarter to seven. I'm supposed to be meeting Seth at seven. Although he did say "seven*ish*." Still, I need to think fast if this is going to work. Rory is all over Imogen like a rash, but she seems to be coping so I tell her I'll make a cup of coffee and leave them in the living room. In the kitchen I quickly send a text to Seth: *Can you meet me outside the nursing home at the end of George Street?*

I go back into the living room. Rory is showing Imogen his boring set of Pokémon cards. With any luck Seth will text me back immediately. The next few minutes take hours to go by while I do my best to look relaxed. Suddenly my phone beeps and there's a text from Seth. I look at the screen.

Be there in ten.

Bloody hell! He must live fairly close, then, I think wildly.

"It's from Mum," I tell Imogen. "She's forgotten something. She wants me to take it to her," I lie. "Do you mind looking after Rory for a bit while I pop down to the nursing home? I don't know how long I'll be . . . I might have to sit with Miss Maybrooke for a while."

I'm worried that Rory is going to kick up a fuss, but he looks quite happy at the prospect of having Imogen all to himself.

Imogen shrugs. "Go ahead," she says. "We'll be all right, won't we, Rory?" He's snuggled up to her on the sofa and as I leave the room I hear him asking her if she'll read him a story. I feel a pang of something. Could it be jealousy? Of what, exactly? That Rory likes Imogen so much or that she likes him? So what? I tell myself crossly. Why should it matter? I should be grateful under the circumstances, shouldn't I? I check myself in the hall mirror before I leave. It's freezing outside but there's no way I'm going to ruin the effect of my new top by covering it up with a big coat.

I pace up and down in front of the nursing home for what seems like an eternity, glancing up at the windows now and again to make sure no one I know spots me. I wonder if I should have just come home without Imogen and told Seth that there was a family emergency and that I couldn't make it tonight. But then all that work making me look nice would have been wasted and the thought of not seeing him when I've been looking forward to it for days would have been too depressing. I could have explained the situation to him and asked him if he wanted to come around and keep me company. Some date that would have been! Rory would have been a pain in the butt and then Mum might have come back and I'd have had to explain him to her. Then she would have given me the lecture about going out with boys who were nearly seventeen and I'm only fourteen (it would be hopeless pointing out to her that I'm nearly fifteen) and why can't I go out with someone nearer my own age. (Like two years is much—Dad's three years older than her—and look at the age gap between him and Trish), but she'd just say that was different and I'd be shouting by this point and saying, "Have you *seen* a fourteen-year-old boy recently? They're not even human!"

I'm so busy playing out this imaginary argument in my head that I don't realize Seth has come up behind me and when he puts his hands over my eyes and says, "Hi, Gorgeous," I very nearly stamp on his foot and elbow him in the stomach like we were taught in self-defense classes. Luckily I don't, and he takes his hands away and I turn around and I stand there staring at him, and he's so lovely I could eat him, and I'm suddenly glad that I told all those lies so that I could see him. I know it sounds really corny but I actually go weak at the knees and have to sit on the wall. He sits down next to me.

"So what do you want to do, then? Why are we meeting here?" he asks, looking around. I can see his point. I decide at that moment to be completely truthful with him. I explain about Mum's emergency and me having to babysit and that I've left Imogen alone at my house watching my little brother for me and that I will have to get back and I'm really sorry, but maybe we could meet up tomorrow or something. I'm babbling because I'm nervous, but it's such a relief to finally be telling the truth to someone. I can't believe it when he starts laughing.

"What?" I ask him. "What's so funny?" and he explains that he's in exactly the same situation and that he shouldn't be out either because he's supposed to be keeping an eye on his stepsister. We sit there grinning at each other and I can tell he's reluctant to go.

"I'm sure she'll be fine for an hour, though," he says.

"I think I could get away with about an hour," I tell him.

"Come on, then. Let's go to the park," and he grabs my hand and pulls me off the wall and we run down the road. He shows me a way into the park where the railings are bent and we squeeze through the gap.

It's a bit spooky in here at night and I don't know if Seth realizes I'm a bit scared or whether he is as well, but he takes hold of my hand and we wander across the grass toward the swings. I'm very aware of his hand in mine and how much pressure to put into the hold. I don't want my hand to be floppy in case he thinks I don't want it held, but then I don't want to hold on too tight and make it uncomfortable. God! Stop stressing and try to enjoy the moment, I tell myself, but I know that in the back of my mind I'm storing up how everything feels so that I can remember it later.

We sit on the swings and chat for a bit. I know I sound all relaxed and calm but my insides are churning with nervousness. I know it's silly but I'm panicking about him kissing me, which obviously he isn't about to do because he's sitting on the next swing. I actually really want him to kiss me, but at the same time I'm dreading it in case I do it all wrong. Suddenly he jumps off the swing and runs over to the merry-go-round.

"Come on," he calls, "I'll push you."

And that's where I get my first kiss, spinning around on a kids' merry-go-round. He pushes it as fast as it will go and jumps on to the seat beside me, and when I turn to smile at him, he leans in and our lips meet and I wonder what exactly it was I was worried about because it feels so wonderful. And if anything does go wrong I can blame it on the fact that we're spinning around. But nothing goes wrong. Our teeth don't clash, our lips aren't too soggy—his are all warm and soft—our noses don't get tangled up and he doesn't try to stick his tongue down my throat, which I realize is the part I was most dreading. In fact, it's perfect, and I know I'll remember this moment for the rest of my life. As we're sitting there, joined at the lips, the merry-go-round slows down, and I wonder if I ought to pull away and what to say, if anything. I hope there isn't going to be an embarrassed silence. I open my eyes, because I've had them shut, and he pulls away and smiles. I don't know if he's about to say something or go back in for another kiss, because at that moment his phone rings.

I'm really hoping he'll ignore it and kiss me again, but he sighs and gets it out of his pocket. I can hear some pretty frantic babbling on the other end.

"Okay. Just calm down . . . I'm coming." Seth takes hold of my hand again and says, "Do you mind running? I really have to get back. There's a gap in the fence at the other side of the park, nearer to where I live. My stepsister is in a right state."

By now we're trotting across the grass.

"I'll just check on her and then I'll walk you home."

Of course I'm aware of the fact that I should be getting back myself, but I don't want to walk across the park on my own and if I leave now I won't get another kiss because Seth is in such a hurry. It just feels wrong to be going in the opposite direction, and

I'm beginning to worry about leaving Imogen for so long, although we were only in the park for about half an hour. I'll make it up to her when I get back by ordering an extra-large pizza.

"God, I'll kill her if this is nothing. I bet she's just trying to ruin my evening," he says as we squeeze through the gap.

But when we get to his house, it's immediately obvious that there's something very wrong. The front door is wide open and there are loads of people in the front garden. It's a huge house and it looks very familiar somehow.

A group of about six boys are shouting a football chant at the tops of their voices and I really don't want to go up the path, but Seth still has hold of my hand as he charges through the crowd and in at the front door.

And that's when the penny drops. I recognize the house because this is where Sasha lives. I have just walked into Sasha's birthday party. Sasha is Seth's new stepsister. My brain is computing these facts quite dispassionately while the rest of it is taking in what's happening. The whole house has been trashed. I don't need to see it all to realize that. I can see into the living room where most of the noise is coming from: loud music, people jumping all over the sofa and chairs, couples joined together—I have to avert my eyes. Not that I'm a prude or anything. Well, maybe I am a bit because I'm sure I'll never do those things in public. Seth is practically tearing his hair out.

I spot some girls from my class at school. Lucy and Miranda, Anna, Jade, and Luke all traipse past me. They're heading for the front door. I don't blame them and have an overwhelming urge to follow, but I can't just run out and leave Seth on his own. There's a couple propped up against the wall, kissing. Seth grabs the girl by the elbow and pulls her out of the embrace.

"Where is she? Where's Sasha?" shouts Seth over the music.

The girl points to a closed door down the corridor. I look a bit closer. Bloody hell! It's Stephanie Young and Henry Trotter: two of the geekiest, shyest people in my class, and I wonder vaguely how they managed to kiss with so much metalwork in their mouths.

Then I realize that they're both extremely drunk. In fact, Henry is looking a bit green, like he's about to throw up.

I suddenly realize that I can't be here. I have to get out before Sasha sees me. Apart from the fact she'll accuse me of crashing, I know for a fact that she'll never forgive me for seeing her humiliation and what happened to her precious party. As I grab hold of Seth to tell him that I'm going to have to go, I spot a security box on the wall behind him.

"Is that a burglar alarm?" I yell. He nods, distractedly. I've just had a brilliant idea. If the alarm goes off everyone will leave the house. "Can you set it off?" I ask him.

"I think so," he says, and starts fiddling with the buttons. I go into the living room and locate the source of the loud music, then turn it off. There's an awful few moments when everyone turns and stares at me and I just want the floor to open up and swallow me. Then the alarm goes off in the silence and everyone jumps, but nobody makes a dash for the door. Instead, the racket seems to make them even more excited. What was I expecting? That they'd think it was a fire alarm and all file out neatly like at school? I'm definitely losing it, but it does give me another idea.

"Fire!" I yell at the top of my voice, but nobody takes any notice.

Then Seth sticks his head around the door and yells at the top of his voice, "POLICE!" It certainly does the trick and the cry of "Police!" goes up everywhere, spreading through the house as fast as a socially unacceptable disease. There's a mad dash for the door with people pushing and shoving, until eventually nearly everyone's gone. The burglar alarm stops and there's an ominous silence.

"Now why didn't I think of that?" I say to Seth.

He looks really miserable. "The police will come out. They always do when the alarm goes off. That's why we're not supposed to touch it."

"Well, it was an emergency," I say, looking around the room. And it definitely looks like they've been burgled. I can't believe the extent of the destruction. It's not just a mess that can be sorted out by a quick tidy-up. Things have been destroyed.

Someone has tried to smash the glass-topped coffee table. It's got cracks radiating out from the point where it was hit by—I'm guessing—a beer bottle, which is lying on the carpet underneath. In fact, someone's been around the room smashing everything in sight—the glass in the picture frames and the doors of a display cabinet that holds Sasha's mum's porcelain figure collection.

As I pick my way through the debris on the floor toward the cabinet, I remember playing in this room with Sasha when we were little. It's funny, but I never really think about how we were friends when we were little. At some point, when we'd just started school until we were about seven, we were best friends. We'd gaze at the figures for hours, making up names and lives for them. The case was always locked and we weren't allowed to handle them. Luckily the case is still locked and although most of the figures have fallen over they appear to be undamaged. I can't remember what happened to make me and Sasha fall out, but I guess that's just kids for you.

I check the time. It's just past eight o'clock. That means Imogen has been on her own (if you don't count Rory—which I don't) for over an hour. I really have got to get back. I poke my head around the living room door to check that the coast is clear. It is, so I make a dash for it, but before I get to the front door a load of people flood out of the room, the one Stephanie said Sasha had locked herself in. They all spill out into the hallway and before any of them catch sight of me, I dive through the nearest door, which I'm pretty sure is the downstairs bathroom. Sure enough, it is, but I'm not alone. Henry is leaning into the toilet bowl and Stephanie is perched beside him rubbing his back. I put my fingers to my lips, but they're so wrapped up in themselves that they don't seem to be bothered that a third person is squashed in there with them. There's a disgusting smell of puke and I open the door a crack and peer through the gap, as much to get some air as to see what's going on in the hall.

Sasha's out there, surrounded by a group of her friends. She's obviously been crying, and who can blame her. She is going to be in *so* much trouble. I almost feel sorry for her. *Almost.*

Suddenly Seth comes down the stairs. "I've called our parents," he tells Sasha. "They're on their way home. Has anyone seen Alice?"

No, no, no!

"Alice! What, you mean you brought Alice here?" Sasha is screeching in a most unattractive way.

Seth disappears into the living room and I can hear Chelsea saying to Sasha, "I thought you didn't invite Alice," and then Clara chips in with, "Is Seth going out with *Alice*?"

There's something very uncomfortable about hearing people talk about you when they don't know you're there. I consider just making a dash for the front door now Sasha knows I'm here, anyway. I really need to get home. But I freeze when I hear what Sasha says next.

"Of course not, stupid. But I did have a bet with him that he couldn't get into her pants. He was probably trying to win that. He didn't have to bring her here, though."

If the toilet wasn't already taken I'd probably have turned around and been sick right into it. Luckily, at that moment, everyone in the hall moves off toward the kitchen so at last I can make my getaway. I have to struggle with the front door because I'm blinded by tears, but I get it open and slam it behind me. As I run down the path, I hear the front door open again and Seth's voice calling me. The bastard. How dare he? Is he hoping I'll go back so that he can get into my pants and win his bloody bet? I keep running until I get home.

Chapter Ten

Before I open the front door and apologize to Imogen for taking so long, I try and compose myself a bit. If she sees that I've been crying I'll just pretend that I'm upset about Miss Maybrooke.

But when I get inside I can hear voices in the living room. Damn, I think as I open the door, I'll have to put Rory to bed. But it's not Imogen and Rory in there. It's Imogen and Mum!

They both turn and stare at me. Why is it that everyone seems to be staring at me tonight? Then Mum goes ballistic.

"Where have you been?! I was about to call the police. You're a thoughtless, selfish girl! As if I haven't got enough on my plate!"

This is typical. My mother thinks that she is the only person in the world with problems.

"Imogen says you told her I called you and you had to go to the nursing home. I think you've got some explaining to do."

Hell! I don't know what to say. I glance at Imogen, but she's just staring blankly at the television screen, which is a bit odd as the TV isn't even on. I'm desperately trying to come up with a solution to my lie having been discovered and I'm just contemplating saying that I really wanted to go and see how Miss Maybrooke was doing but was too embarrassed to admit it to Imogen, so I made up the bit about Mum calling. However, even I can see that this was a bit weak as excuses go, and doesn't account for the fact that I've been gone for nearly two hours and never even turned up at the nursing home.

But as I'm wondering what to say, Mum goes off on one. I don't think I've ever seen her so angry. It's like a dam bursting. She starts off with how hard she's tried to keep the family together and hold down a job. This is a bit rich, I think, as it was her who left Dad, which is hardly keeping the family together. Then it's on to me and how selfish I am and how I do nothing to help her and that it's about time I grew up and realized that not everything revolves around me. . . . I won't bore you with all the details. Normally I'd butt in and have a go back at her about how it's not me that's selfish, it's her, for ruining my life, etc., etc., but like I said, I've never seen her so angry and I can't get a word in. Also, it's really embarrassing because Imogen is sitting there having to listen to the whole tirade.

The only good thing is that Mum seems to have forgotten about the tiny question of where I have actually been. By now she's close to tears and is trying really hard not to cry. It turns out she got to the nursing home just in time, because Miss Maybrooke passed away shortly after she got there.

"Not only have I just lost a very dear friend and could have done without coming home to your thoughtlessness, but don't forget that this house belonged to her and there's a very real possibility that we could soon be homeless."

After this devastating announcement, Mum rushes from the room, no doubt because she can no longer hold back the tears.

I feel completely drained. Too much has happened this evening and none of it is good. Well, the kiss from Seth was good at the time, but now I know his real motive it is ruined forever in my mind. Everything is ruined. My whole life is a complete disaster.

I flop down on to the sofa next to Imogen. Why, oh why did I invite her back here! Why didn't I just accept, at the beginning, that my evening was ruined instead of making it so much worse? If I'd just come home I'd be sitting in my room now, wishing that I'd been able to go out with Seth but blissfully unaware about what a rat he is. It strikes me that Imogen is being very quiet and I suddenly feel bad about her having to witness all that.

"Sorry about my mum," I say. "She doesn't half go on."

Still nothing from Imogen, only silence. I steal a quick look at her, then wish I hadn't. I've never seen anything so scary. She's clutching a cushion and her knuckles are white where she's gripping it so tightly. She looks too angry to speak, which is just as well because I don't think I can take any more tonight. I'm just wondering if I should suggest that she calls her dad to come and get her when she turns to me.

"I can't believe how you've *used* me." This is forced out between clenched teeth, and I involuntarily cringe back into the corner of the sofa.

"You planned this right from the start, didn't you? You got me here so you could sneak out. I bet you were meeting that boy from the Sixth Form. Don't give me any more lies," she adds as I open my mouth to defend myself. "I've had to spend the last week watching you mooning around after him like some dumb-struck idiot. And to think I spent the whole afternoon helping you to get ready! What were you going to do? Pretend that you had to go home and go and meet him when you were supposed to be at my house?"

I can feel myself going red as she hits on the truth. We had actually had a really good time today, shopping and doing my makeover, but now my ulterior motive has been uncovered it does seem like I was just using Imogen.

Although a part of me feels really bad, there's another part that is angry. If Imogen was any kind of friend I could have told her about my date. I could have asked her to cover for me and everything we did this afternoon would have been her helping me and supporting me. So it's not my fault, it's hers—for not understanding.

Okay, so I didn't tell her what was happening and that I had a date and give her a chance to help me, but somehow I just knew that she'd be dismissive of the whole thing and tell me I was wasting my time with him. It doesn't help that she would have been right either. Perhaps I ought to point this out to her. It doesn't look like I'm going to get a chance, though, because Imogen hasn't finished yet on "the failings of Alice Watkins."

"Your mum's right. You are selfish. All you ever think about is yourself. You're always going on about how terrible your life is, but you don't know how lucky you are. If you think your life is horrible, you ought to try mine."

I know my mouth is hanging open, but I can't seem to close it. What is Imogen going on about? How could she side with my mum? What does she mean, *lucky?*

"At least you've got a mum and dad," I say, "and you live in a nice house, so I don't know what you're complaining about."

"Big bloody deal!" Imogen says. "You live in a nice house and you have a mum and a dad, they just happen to be divorced. Well, I wish my parents were divorced; then I wouldn't have to put up with both of them. All they care about is each other. I don't even know why they bothered having me—I just get in their way. All they do is slobber over each other—it's sick! I feel like a bloody lodger! In my own home! Except it isn't a home and we're not a family and I can't wait to get out of there."

Imogen is nearly in tears now and I don't know what to say. Then I remember earlier when I was thinking about her and her mum.

"But your mum," I tell her, "at least you've got something in common with her. You know—her being an artist and everything." If I was hoping that this would cheer Imogen up, I couldn't have been further off the mark.

"My mum's not a bloody artist," spits Imogen. "Just because she thinks she is doesn't make her one. Throwing paint at a canvas doesn't make you an artist." Imogen's voice is oozing contempt. "You know, my mum can't even draw. She hates the fact that I can draw—she hates the stuff I do—the manga and my sketchbooks. She hates ME! I just get in the way of her precious life and her self-obsession."

I'm amazed. I've always been jealous of Imogen's life; the fact that she doesn't have an annoying brother and that her parents are still together and that she has such a nice bedroom and everything. But if it's true about her mum then I don't blame her for wanting to go away to boarding school.

I'm just thinking about apologizing to Imogen and sympathizing with her and promising to be a better friend but I don't get the chance. She's standing up now and pointing an accusing finger at me.

"If you stopped to look, you'd see how great your mum really is," Imogen is going on. "At least she cares about you, and if you weren't so horrible to her all the time and tried to help instead of making everything more difficult for her, then you might realize that there's nothing wrong with your life except YOU. Why are you so angry all the time? You're horrid to your little brother and I don't know why you hate him because he's actually really cute. I'd give anything to have a little brother or a mum that cared about me." She's practically shouting now.

I jump up off the sofa and face her. "How dare you presume to know what my life is like!" I yell.

I'm really mad now because she's supposed to be my friend and she's starting to sound exactly like my mum. In fact, I'm about to point this out to her when Mum comes back in. She's obviously been crying about Miss Maybrooke and she must have also had time to think because she says to me, apparently oblivious to the fact that Imogen and I have been shouting at each other, "You still haven't explained to me where you went."

Imogen folds her arms across her chest and glowers at me. "Yes, where did you go?"

This is too much. Way, way too much.

"I'm waiting for an answer, young lady." I hate it when Mum calls me that. They're both standing there, staring at me. I really have had enough of people staring accusingly at me for one day.

"I'll tell you where I went. I went to meet a *friend*." As I emphasise the last word I stare directly at Imogen. She makes a sort of snorting noise through her nose as if to say, "Yeah, right!"

"Friend? What friend?" demands Mum. I'm not about to tell her, but I decide to let Imogen know what happened.

"I met my friend, but they were supposed to be looking after their stepsister—who was having a party," I explain, desperately trying to avoid the *he* word. "Anyway, some *idiot*"—again I glare at Imogen—"advertised the party on the Internet and all these party crashers turned up and trashed the house and we had to go there and get rid of them. . . ."

I'm going to carry on but Mum, as usual, completely misses the point and says in her "incredulous" voice, "Are you telling me that you left Imogen here—on her own—to watch Rory, while you went to a *party*¿! And didn't even tell her where you were going¿"

"I didn't go to a party!" I yell at Mum. "I went to meet a friend. Someone who . . ." I'm about to say "someone who's really nice to me, and understands me, and likes me and isn't about to abandon me and we had a really good time," but then I remember the bet and the reason for Seth being there and being "really nice" and that's when I finally lose it and burst into tears. I don't mean I have tears falling gracefully down my cheeks, I mean great, ugly, gut-wrenching sobs.

"I knew it," says Imogen. "You went to meet that boy."

"What boy¿" says Mum.

"He's in the Sixth Form—" begins Imogen. That does it. She's colluding with my mum and I don't think I'm ever going to forgive her.

"I hate you! I hate you both!" I scream. Not very original, I know, but I'm under pressure here. I storm out into the hall and grab my coat. Mum's followed me out.

"Where do you think—" she begins, but I open the front door and yell at her, "I'm going to Dad's. I'm going to *live* at Dad's," and I slam the door so hard that the stained glass rattles. It opens again as I get to the gate.

"Alice! Come back here—" I don't wait for the "immediately." Instead I slam the gate as hard as I can, so the broken latch rattles, and glare at my mother over the top.

"Never!" I shout, copying Rory's favorite retort, and run down the road.

I'm running down the same streets that I ran down earlier

with Seth, only then I felt happy and full of nervous excitement. Now I feel . . . I don't know . . . everything opposite. Angry, very angry. I never want to see Imogen or my mum ever again. I hate them. I don't care that I've argued with Imogen. What does it matter now she's not going to be here, anyway. Maybe I can swap schools when I'm living with Dad. Then I can just start again.

This thought actually cheers me up a little bit. I'm worried that they'll be following me, though, so when I get to the hole in the park railings I squeeze through and push my way through the undergrowth. I'm still scared, like I was earlier. It does occur to me that to enter the park at night—alone—is not the action of a sane person, but as I'm not feeling particularly sane at the moment, I don't care. I'm still so angry. If a pervert jumped out of the bushes and attacked me, I'd very probably kill him.

All I have to do is call Dad and get him to come and pick me up. The only problem is I've only got his home number and it's half past nine on a Saturday night so he's bound to be in the pub. As I get my phone and dial his number, I pray that married life has changed him and that he's sitting cozily at home with his new wife.

I'm expecting the phone to ring and ring, but it's snatched up immediately.

"Gary? Is that you?" It's Trish and she sounds funny.

"It's Alice. Is Dad there?" A stupid question really. Obviously he's not there or why would she think he was calling her?

"No."

I wait for her to expand on this, but there's just a silence on the other end.

"Will he be back soon?"

Again, "No."

"Can you give me his cell number?"

"No."

This is getting weird. I really don't need this. I just want my dad.

"Trish, I really need to talk to him. It's an emergency. Just give me his number . . . please."

"There's no point. He hasn't got it switched on."

"But I really need to talk to him." I'm squeaking now.

"You and me both. I haven't heard from him for two days."

"What do you mean? Has he gone away on business?"

Trish starts laughing. I hold the phone away from my ear, but even from there I can hear the hysterical note in that laugh. All the time I've been talking to her I've been walking and now I've reached the playground. I perch on the edge of the merry-go-round and put the phone back to my ear. There is a strange sound coming from the other end. The laughing is punctuated by sobs and then there is no more laughter, just sobbing.

"I can't believe I've been so stupid." Trish is raving. I don't think she's even talking to me, she's just going on. "I should have known . . . I mean, I know he hates kids . . . I knew that . . . The way he's always complaining about the ones he's got . . . Why didn't I listen . . . I thought it would be different . . . I thought it would be all right if *we* had one . . . and now look . . . he's left me. He said he thought I didn't want a baby . . . that I was too taken up with my career . . . but I did . . . I do . . . I do want this baby . . . I thought it was going to be okay . . . I mean he married me, didn't he? And then when I started buying things for the baby . . . he just . . . and now he's GONE."

"What do you mean he's gone? I need to talk to him!"

"Haven't you been listening? I'm pregnant, and he's left me."

"Yes, but where is he?"

"I DON'T KNOW!"

Now I'm crying as well. I was going to go to Dad's and now he's not there. I can't go home. No way.

"Trish? Can I come over?"

"What?"

"I was going to ask Dad if I could come and live with you."

"What!?"

"The thing is . . . I can't live at home anymore . . . I could help you with the baby . . ."

"What, like you *help* with Rory?" I don't like the way she says *help*, like I never do. That is so unfair.

"But this will be different . . ."

"How will it be different? I'll tell you how it will be different. I'll be the single mother of two. Not only will I have to look after a baby on my own, I'll also have a selfish, self-obsessed teenager to cope with as well."

"But I'll help you!"

"You don't know the meaning of the word! The only person you've ever helped is yourself. You're just like your dad. Well, I'll tell you something. I don't want to have anything to do with him anymore, which means I never have to see you again either. I never want to hear the name Watkins again. I'm going to give the baby *my* surname. If you want to go and live with your dad, fine! You deserve each other. That is if you can find him! Don't you dare come here. I won't be here, anyway. I'm going to my mum's."

And she hangs up on me! The cow. Why was she saying all those horrible things to me?

I'm still crying. I just sit there letting the tears roll down my face. It's very quiet. I'm not so scared anymore, though. Nobody in their right mind would be out in the park tonight. It's freezing. Of course, I'm not in my right mind, which is why I'm here.

I'm surprised the tears aren't freezing on my face. I haven't got any gloves. I'll probably get frostbite. In fact, I'll probably freeze to death, because I'm not going home. I'll just have to stay here in the park. They'll find my frozen body in the morning. Then they'll be sorry.

I hate them all. I hate my life. I hate me. I hate Seth. Sitting here on the merry-go-round where I got my first proper kiss, I think back to how it was. He ought to get an Oscar for his performance. I really thought he liked me. I thought we were having a great time together. How could he have kissed me like that and not meant it? I feel so humiliated.

It was a great kiss, though. I jump off the merry-go-round and start to push it around until it's going as fast as I can get it. I hop on and sit there trying to remember the kiss. I shut my eyes.

He leaned in and our lips met. His lips were lovely and warm even though his nose was cold. Mmmm. It was nice. Bastard!

Suddenly I'm aware that the merry-go-round isn't slowing down. It ought to be. I open my eyes and twist around to see if someone has sneaked up on me and is pushing it. For a moment I almost expect to see Seth—grinning at me.

There's nobody there, but the merry-go-round is getting faster! I think about jumping off, but I daren't. I'm clinging on to the rail trying not to get thrown off. And then a seriously freaky thing happens. The merry-go-round stops spinning. I know this because I don't have to hold on anymore as I'm not being pulled toward the edge by the force. The only problem is everything else continues to spin. The park and the sky and the moon and the stars are all spinning madly around the merry-go-round. I'm beginning to feel sick. And then the merry-go-round starts spinning again in the opposite direction to the rest of the world, and I'm taken by surprise at how fast it speeds up. I don't get a firm enough hold on the rail and I'm slipping and I can't hold on. I feel myself being flung off the merry-go-round and I'm waiting to hit the ground only it seems to be taking forever, and while I'm waiting I'm seeing all the people that I hate—Mum and Imogen and Rory and Seth and Sasha and Dad and Trish—and then nothing.

PART 2

Chapter One

The first thing I notice is that it's daytime and sunny. It should be dark. I mean, it was about nine-thirty in the evening when I got into the park. Now I'm lying on the ground under a blue sky and the sun is shining. Was I knocked out? Have I been lying here all night?

Gingerly, I move my head and then my arms and legs to see if anything hurts. It doesn't—I feel fine. In fact, I feel more than fine. I feel great. I sit up but something isn't right. I'm wearing a dress, for starters, and socks—white knee-high ones. How strange. My feet are in sandals, the sort that young children wear. I wiggle my toes. The toes wiggle. But they can't be my feet, they're way too small. Then I see the braids hanging down. Why is my hair in braids? I tug at them. Ouch—yes, they're definitely mine. I stand up. The ground is too near, like I've shrunk or something.

Beyond the swings is a slide. It's one of those tube slides made out of stainless steel. In other words, I'll be able to see my reflection in it. I begin to run toward it and fall flat on my face. I pick myself up and walk. Obviously I need a bit of time to get used to my new shape. I feel much lighter and looser. Sort of springy and bouncy.

I peer into the metal side of the slide. The reflection is distorted because of the way the tube curves, but I can see myself well enough. Or I would be able to, if there wasn't some snotty kid in the way. I look around to tell her to scoot, but there's no one there. I'm alone. I turn back to the slide, and there's the kid again. It's me! It's a little me!

My face is rounder and my nose much smaller. What I'm looking at is me when I was about seven or eight. I sit down on the end of the slide where the tube comes out onto a flattened part. My heart is flibberty flobbing. Must breathe.

The metal feels warm against the back of my bare legs—my now very skinny legs. I notice a graze covering most of my left knee. Did I do that when I came flying off the merry-go-round? It looks quite old, all crusty and scabbed over. I pick at the scab and a bit of it flakes off easily, leaving the skin underneath all pink and shiny and new. I put the end of one of my braids into my mouth and suck. I need to think.

I haven't sucked my hair for years. It's such a familiar sensation, but a far-off memory at the same time. I must concentrate; I need to process what's happening here. Something very weird—that's for sure. I must be hallucinating. That's it! I fell off the merry-go-round and hit my head and now I'm hallucinating.

I shut my eyes and shake my head vigorously. I'll be okay in a minute, I know I will. Please, please, please let it be okay. When I open my eyes, though, everything's just the same: The dress, the sandals, the scab, the braids—they're all still there. If I'm hallucinating, it's very realistic.

I can see some people coming across the grass toward the playground. It's a group of three mothers and five children and I decide it's time to go. There's nothing for it—I'll have to go home and face my mum. To be truthful, all I want at the moment is to go home. I don't care if Mum shouts at me. If I've been out all night she'll think I've been at Dad's. If she called him to check, she wouldn't have got any answer, not now that Trish has gone to her mum's. I wonder if I ought to tell Mum about the baby and Dad disappearing?

I have this feeling that once I get home, everything will be all right—I'll tell Mum I'm not well and go to bed and go to sleep and then when I wake up this nightmare will be over. Of course, I'll still have the nightmare of being betrayed by Seth, and Imogen not speaking to me, and being grounded for evermore, and worrying about where Dad's got to—but hey!—what's all that compared to this? Surely there must be some medical term for thinking you're a child again? Oh yes, it's called insanity.

I start to run. It feels amazing. I haven't run like this for years. At school, in the summer, we have to do cross-country running, but nobody except the keen, sporty ones actually *runs*. Most of us just lope around the course, jogging for a bit, but mostly walking.

Now, I'm flying across the grass—I feel like I could go on forever—that my legs will carry me to the ends of the earth if I asked them to. And maybe they would, but I run out of breath before I reach the gates, and have to stop.

I do a couple of cartwheels. Wow, it's easy! I try a handstand. Then I realize I'm showing my underwear. There's a man and a dog walking along the path and I look at him to see if he's noticed. He smiles at me and his dog comes running over, wagging its tail, and starts licking me. The man follows and takes the dog by the collar, pulling it away.

"Where's your mummy?" he asks, looking around, no doubt for a responsible adult. Now, I try not to believe that *every* man is a pervert, and I'm sure this man means well, but the truth is you can't tell just by looking at someone if they're okay or not, so I decide to get out of there.

"She's in the bathroom," I tell him and run off toward the restrooms.

The public restrooms in the park aren't very nice, and normally I'd try not to use them. Luckily, they are empty and I run over to the mirrors to check if I'm back to normal, but they're too high up and I can't see. I scramble up onto the sink unit. Damn, I still look seven. I poke my tongue out at myself and grin. Oh, my God! I've got two teeth missing. Did that happen when I fell off the merry-go-round?

This is a disaster! My two front teeth—gone! I can't go around like this! I've got to get to a dentist. Hang on, my teeth aren't the only things that feel odd.

With my heart racing, I climb down and shut myself in one of the toilet cubicles. I lift up my dress and see a pair of pink underwear. They've got a picture of Barbie on them. Okay—I think—this is definitely some weird hallucination. I peek inside. Eeek! All my pubic hair has fallen out. I look up top. Obviously I'm not wearing a bra—there's nothing there. I'm completely flat! I can see my ribs.

Then I realize something. The man out there, with the dog, asked me where my "mummy" was. He must have seen a seven-year-old girl as well. So it can't all be in my head. Unless he was hallucinating, too—which is ridiculous. Maybe he was part of my hallucination. This all started when I flew off that stupid merry-go-round so maybe, in reality, I'm lying in intensive care, in a coma, imagining all this. I pinch myself. Ouch!

I leave the bathroom and start to run again. When I turn into George Street everything looks beautifully normal. Usually, when I approach number twelve, a feeling of depression descends upon me because the house looks so unwelcoming. There's a huge yew hedge surrounding the front garden and this cuts out most of the sunshine. The grass is all mossy, hardly anything can grow in there, and the front path is always slimy and wet. Today, though, I don't care. I push open the front gate. It isn't as rickety as usual—Mum must have had it fixed.

I skid up the front path and realize that I haven't got my front-door key on me. I'll have to see if the back door's open. I go around the side of the house but for some reason the side gate's closed, and when I try to open it, I find it's locked. We never shut that gate and I didn't even know Mum had a key for it. I go back to the front door and ring the bell. If Mum has a go at me for forgetting my key I'll just shout at her for locking the side gate. Why is she taking so long to come to the door? I can see her through the stained glass, making her way down the hall. God! Why is she so slow?

I'm bouncing up and down with impatience. Finally, she's at the door. Now she's fiddling with the safety chain! We never use that. God, hurry up! The door opens and I'm about to shout at her for being so slow, but the words get sucked back in by my gasp. Because, instead of Mum standing there, it's Miss Maybrooke. The Miss Maybrooke that was at death's door only last night—the Miss Maybrooke who called for Mum to dash to her bedside— thereby ruining my date with Seth and, in fact, my life.

Is this some sort of elaborate joke that Mum has cooked up? Is she trying to get her own back because I scared her last night by going out and not telling her where I was? No, that's crazy. Miss Maybrooke was ill. She was bedridden. I saw her myself at the nursing home. But this is definitely her standing at the door, and although she's old and bent she isn't *dead*. When Mum got home last night she was upset because Miss Maybrooke had died. She'd never joke about something like that.

"Can I help you, dear?"

I realize I'm doing my guppy impression again—the one I did when Luke asked me out—the one where I stand there with my mouth opening and closing.

"You're a bit young to be working for social services. They said they'd send someone around to help me with the housework. I was expecting someone a bit older. You're not from social services, surely?"

"No," I say and then, in a moment of inspiration, "I'm from the Girl Scouts . . . no, the Brownies." Am I seven or fourteen? I don't care—I just want to get inside the house to see if Mum and Rory are in there. "It's 'Bob a Job' week. Do you have any jobs you'd like me to do?"

Miss Maybrooke looks doubtful.

"Well, I don't know, dear. You look a bit small."

That's right, rub it in, I think.

"Maybe I can find something for you to do. You'd better come in so I can shut the door and keep the cold out." I'm tempted to tell her that it's a hot, sunny day beyond the hedge and that she should chop it down—but what's the point? She's only a hallucination.

She moves aside and I step indoors. The first thing that I notice is the smell. It smells of lavender and beeswax with an undertone of old lady. Also, there's linoleum on the hall floor. It's all grubby and cracked. The air is cold and damp. If I thought it was bad when I lived here, this is much worse.

By now we've reached the kitchen, but instead of the bright new one my mum had fitted, it's really old-fashioned and it smells of sour milk. Now I know it's not a joke.

Miss Maybrooke is rummaging under the sink and pulls out a bag of potatoes. She spreads some newspaper on the table and hands me a potato peeler.

"I wonder if you could do these for me. I have a bit of trouble with them these days, with my hands like this." She waves them at me and I see that they're all scrunched up—the fingers twisted and bent. "Arthritis," she says. "It's a terrible thing, getting old."

You ought to try getting younger, I think. It's not exactly a bundle of laughs. I'm having trouble keeping hold of the potato because my hands aren't big enough.

"I think I've got some orange punch somewhere." She's rummaging in the cupboard again and brings out a sticky-looking bottle containing something dangerously orange. She pours some into a glass and gives it to me. I take a tentative sip and try not to spit it back out all over the potatoes. Should I tell her that it's supposed to have water added to it? Now she's found me some carrots and as I peel them, I wonder about discussing my problem with her. But what exactly could I say? "I had an accident and I'm in a coma and not really here," sounds like the ramblings of a deranged person. She's likely to think that it's just some game I'm playing.

It's then that I notice the newspaper. I push aside the peelings and look for the date.

"Is this today's paper?" I ask as innocently as possible, trying to keep the excitement out of my voice.

"No, dear, that's yesterday's. I haven't read today's yet."

And there it is, at the top—June 2, which is right—but seven years ago!

Miss Maybrooke is getting some money out of her purse.

"Thank you, dear, that's very helpful," she says, handing it to me. "You'd better run off home. Where do you live? Is it far?" That is a very good question. If I don't live here—which I obviously don't—then where do I live? Oh, my God! Of course!

"I live at Twenty-five Cavendish Street," I tell her, which is where the seven-year-old me lived. I have to get back there. This is truly awesome—I'm going HOME.

Chapter Two

I run all the way to Cavendish Street. I could get a bus some of the way, with the money I've just earned, but I'm so excited I feel like running. I slow down when I get a couple of streets from home, though. What if I'm wrong? What if Mum isn't at the house in Cavendish Street?

I stop when I get there and stand looking at it. It's just an ordinary house—not old, like Miss Maybrooke's house on George Street. This house has an open front garden, a garage, and a red front door. It looks like home. I've lost count of the number of times I've wished that I still lived here with Mum and Dad and no Rory.

Right, here goes. I ring the front-door bell and when the door opens, there's my mum. She looks perfectly "mumlike," only prettier and happier and a lot taller. No—I forgot; it's me that's a lot shorter. The relief at seeing her is too much and I burst into tears.

"Alice, sweetheart, whatever's the matter?"

She pulls me to her and gives me a huge hug. My first reaction is to pull away. I never hug my mum—I leave that sort of thing to Rory. But somehow it feels right. When I put my arms around her, though, there's a big lump in the way.

"Oops, mind the baby," she says and I realize that she's pregnant and that "the baby" must be Rory.

I manage to reduce my sobbing to sniffing.

"Have you fallen out with Sasha again?" says Mum, looking up and down the street. "Did her mummy just drop you off and go?" She tuts and closes the door. "She could have waited. What if I'd been out or something?"

What? What *is* she talking about?

"Never mind," she continues, "I'm sure you'll make it up with Sasha at school tomorrow."

Of course! When I was seven, Sasha and I were always around each other's houses. I suppose Mum thinks that's where I've been. But never mind all that—I'm here in Cavendish Street!

"Come and have some milk and cookies," says Mum. It's a bit freaky—she's talking to me in the same way that she talks to Rory. We go into the kitchen. I want to run around the house looking at everything and touching it to make sure it's real, but Mum's poured me a glass of milk and put a couple of cookies on a plate. Chocolate cookies.

"I'd rather have a coffee," I say.

Mum laughs. "You funny thing," she says, and gives me a kiss. Okay, I guess coffee's off the menu, then.

"Mum, where's Dad?" I ask her.

"At work, of course," she says.

"But will he be coming back? Here—I mean. He will come home, won't he?"

She gives me a funny look and is about to say something, when the phone rings. "Just a sec, love," and she goes into the hall to answer it.

I look around the kitchen, which is so strange and yet familiar at the same time. There's one of Rory's drawings stuck to the fridge door. Except, of course, it isn't Rory's, I realize—it's mine. I've drawn Mum and Dad, each with one arm stiffly stuck out and in the middle is me, holding their hands.

As I finish my milk and cookies, I can hear Mum on the phone. "Hang on . . . let me find a pen . . . okay . . . Miss Maybrooke . . . yes . . . Twelve George Street . . . Where is that, exactly? Oh, right . . . yes, I know. Tomorrow . . . ten o'clock . . . okay, thanks, bye." She comes back into the kitchen clutching a piece of paper.

"Who was that?" I ask.

"Just work. Social services. They've given me a new old lady to help. I'm going there tomorrow, if I can find it, that is. George Street . . . hmm, I'd better get the map out. I hope she's nice."

This is all completely bizarre. In fact, it's doing my head in. I'm about to tell Mum exactly where George Street is but realize, in this weird world, I'm not supposed to know.

"Mum?" I say.

She looks up. "Goodness, Alice. Have you been playing at being grown-up at Sasha's? What with the coffee and calling me 'Mum' instead of 'Mummy.' I hope I'm not going to lose my little girl too soon." She gives me another hug and a kiss.

I can't take much more of this. "I think I'll go and lie down for a bit."

Suddenly she's all concerned and feeling my forehead and stuff. "Are you feeling all right? I hope you're not coming down with anything. Perhaps you'd better have some Tylenol."

"Look, I'll be fine, okay? I've just got a bit of a headache coming on," I say, and I stomp out of the room. On my way up the stairs, I can see her at the kitchen door watching me in a concerned way. I dash into my bedroom and shut the door.

Oh, my God! I've just entered Barbie Land. Nearly everything in here is pink. The carpet is Barbie-pink, the walls, thankfully, are a few shades paler, but pink all the same. The curtains have Barbie all over them, and the bed is a shrine to Barbie, with its pillowcases and huge picture of Barbie Princess on the duvet cover. Now I really do have a headache. I mean, I know I used to like Barbie and everything—I just didn't realize I'd actually worshipped her.

I move half a dozen Barbie dolls off my bed and climb in. I need to shut my eyes—not only to block out this pink nightmare—but to think. There's no point in thinking how or why this is happening to me. The point is—it *is* happening and I'm living in it. What am I going to do?

I'm just pondering this cataclysmic question when I hear my bedroom door creaking slowly open. If that's Rory, I'll kill him. He knows he's not allowed in my bedroom . . . but of course, it can't be him—he's safely trapped inside my mother. It must be Mum with the Tylenol.

I open my eyes. There's no one there. Then I hear a little meow. I look down—"Sooty!"—and I'm crying again but laughing at the same time. Sooty gives me a look and I can tell he's thinking about leaving, so I jump out of bed and pick him up. I bury my face in his fur and carry him back to the bed. It broke my heart when Sooty died. I think back, madly trying to remember when it was that he got run over. Maybe I can stop it from happening.

And then it hits me! What else could I stop from happening? I run around my bedroom trying to find a piece of paper and a pen. I need to make a list. There's so much going on, I'm sure I'll think straighter if I can write it down. I open a cupboard and a load of cuddly animals and toys fall out. Great. I'm going to have to do something about all this junk, and I definitely need to redecorate in here.

Then I see a box with crayons and coloring books in it. I dig down and find an old notebook and a pencil. Predictably, they've got Barbie plastered all over them. Opening the book, I see I've written two pages of what looks like a story.

Once up on a time there was a princess who lived in a very very very very big castle.

I rip the pages out, crumple them up, and sit down on the bed next to Sooty. Right—things to change.

Now, I know that top of the list should be something like, *Stop the terrorists from blowing up the World Trade Center*, and believe me, I do give it some thought—but how on earth am I going to manage that? I mean, who is going to listen to a fourteen-year-old . . . no, a seven-year-old . . . for heaven's sake? Nobody. And then, I have to admit, to my shame, I don't even know the year that it happened. I'm not proud of myself for this and swear that when things return to normal I will pay more attention to world affairs. Maybe Imogen is right and I don't think about anything but myself.

With a weary sigh I put that thought aside. Back to the present—or what is passing for the present at the moment—if you see what I mean. I write in the pad:

1. Stop Sooty from getting run over.

I'm going to have enough trouble with this without worrying about terrorists.

What can I remember about Sooty getting run over? It must have been the summer, because we buried him in the garden, and I remember Dad had to dig a hole and it was a really hot day. When we put Sooty in the hole, I couldn't stop crying and had to go inside before Dad filled it in. I couldn't stand the thought of all that dirty soil on top of Sooty.

I stroke Sooty behind his ears and he purrs loudly. "Don't worry, Sooty," I tell him, "I'll save you."

Where was Mum when Sooty was being buried? Was she at work? Then I remember. Maybe it's being back here and being small again—but I start remembering things I haven't thought about for years.

While Dad filled in the hole, I went inside and ran up the stairs to Mum and Dad's bedroom because Mum was in bed. I was crying and ran to Mum, expecting her to comfort me. She was sitting up in bed feeding Rory—he must have been a tiny baby—and when I scrambled onto the bed, so Mum could hug me, I startled Rory and he started crying. Then—to my horror—Mum started crying, too. I was frightened because I'd never seen my mum crying before and that made me cry even more. Then my dad walked in and there we were, me and Mum and Rory, all sitting on the bed crying.

I remember what happened next because it was the first time I really hated Rory. Dad said, "Jesus!" and walked out of the room. I ran after him down the stairs and he picked up his pool cue from the umbrella stand. He looked at me, sitting on the stairs and said, "I can't stand all this noise," then he opened the front door and as he left I heard him say, "Bloody babies," before the front door slammed behind him.

After that I always thought of Rory as "the bloody baby," and when he cried I'd creep up to his crib and hiss, "Bloody baby, bloody baby."

I sit on the Barbie bed remembering all this. It was the worst time in my life. I realize, with a sinking feeling, that it looks like I'm going to have to live through it all over again. I've got to stop it from happening. I add to the list:

2. Stop Mum from having Rory.

Then I cross it out. That's hardly going to happen. She's very pregnant. Okay then:

2. Stop Mum and Dad from splitting up.

Suddenly number one looks easy compared to that. The door opens and Mum comes in.

"Haven't you heard of knocking?" I say, quickly hiding the notebook under the pillow. The sarcasm I intended to convey is slightly lost because of my squeaky, seven-year-old voice. Mum looks hurt.

"I just came up to see if you're feeling any better."

"I'm fine, okay?"

"Alice, did something happen to you today—something that upset you—when you were at Sasha's? You can tell me, you know." She moves Sooty off the bed, sits down, and puts her arm around me.

There's so much I want to say and yet I can't. I play a few speeches over in my head:

"Look, Mum—I'm not seven, okay . . . I'm fourteen and I don't appreciate all this attention . . ."

or

"Mum, have you thought about having that baby adopted?"

or

"Don't get divorced and ruin my life and turn into a witch who nags me and makes me babysit all the time so I don't get a life of my own and shouts at me and makes me live in a dark, depressing house on the other side of town . . . and don't give birth to that horrid brat who's responsible for it all . . ."

What I actually end up saying is, "I want to redecorate this room."

"Oh, Alice, I thought you loved it. It's only just been done. We can't do it again until you're at least nine."

"Well, I've gone off it. It stinks. I mean, Barbie, for God's sake!"

"Alice! Don't talk like that. What's wrong with you?" She stands up. Oh no, here we go. She'll probably go off on one about my attitude and how ungrateful I am, etc., etc., but she doesn't. Instead, she looks like a woman whose loved and trusted dog has just bitten her.

"I'll call you when tea's ready," she says, and leaves the room.

I flop back on the bed feeling miserable. Why was I so horrid to my mum just now? She's been nothing but kind to me since I arrived in this nightmare. Is it just a habit I've got into? I might have the mind of a fourteen-year-old, but I'm trapped in the body of a seven-year-old, so by rights I shouldn't have all those mad hormones rushing about inside me—the ones that all adults blame teenagers' bad behavior on. Maybe it's not the hormones that are to blame. Maybe it's just that we grow up and realize that our parents are hopeless losers and that's why we get so mad at them.

Perhaps I ought to try behaving more like a seven-year-old. I decide to practice. I get up off the bed and stand in the middle of the room. What do I do? I skip around the room a couple of times. I feel a bit silly, even though there's no one to see me. I pick up one of the Barbie dolls that I threw on the floor earlier.

"Hello, my name's Barbie."

"Hi, I'm Ken."

They look at each other. I used to play with these for hours. What did I do with them? Ken is eyeing up Barbie, who simpers at him. Suddenly, I start having thoughts about Ken and Barbie that I'm sure no seven-year-old ever had. I throw them across the room. They're just reminding me of Seth and the humiliation of Sasha's party.

I decide to go downstairs. Mum is in the kitchen getting tea ready. I pause in the hall, then push open the kitchen door. Mum looks up and smiles at me.

"How are you feeling, sweetheart?" she asks.

I go over and put my arms around her. It feels a bit awkward, but it seems to make her happy. She strokes my hair.

"I'm sorry, Mum—my." I remember to add on that last bit.

"It's all right, darling. I expect you're just tired. Why don't you go and watch television for a bit until this is ready."

"Okay, Mummy, thanks," I say and go into the living room. It feels so good to be back here, although, to be honest, it is a bit shabbier than I remember. The furniture is definitely second-hand and none of it matches. Still, I make myself comfortable and settle down to watch *Friends*. It's one I haven't seen for ages—an early one—and I'm just getting into it when Mum pokes her head around the door.

"Alice, why on earth are you watching that rubbish? I don't think it's very suitable." She picks up the remote control and changes channels. "Oh, look, *Mary Poppins* is on—that's much better." She smiles and sits down next to me. She's uncomfortably close.

"Hey! I was watching that." Before I realize what I'm doing, I grab the remote out of her hand and turn it back to *Friends*.

Mum stands up, goes over to the television, and turns it off.

"Go up to your room, young lady, and don't come back down until you can behave properly." She's not actually shouting, but I know that look.

"God!" I say, and storm out of the room. I bang my feet as loudly as possible on the stairs and then slam my bedroom door. So much for behaving like a seven-year-old.

It's very quiet in my bedroom. I'm shocked to discover that I'm actually missing Rory. If he was here I could take my frustration out on him. I take the notebook from under my pillow and add:

3. *Find a way to get back to reality.*

Because, I think—until that happens, this is reality.

Chapter Three

I'm in my bedroom reorganizing. Luckily, the Barbie bedding is plain on the inside, so I've turned the pillow and the duvet over, which is a slight improvement. I've piled as many toys as I can into boxes and pushed them under the bed, and I've put all the cuddly toys back in the closet.

That is, all except one. I came across my old bear, called, for some reason that I've forgotten, Mr. Magoo. He had been my childhood friend and went everywhere with me until he got lost— I think I left him on a bus—and never got him back. I was about eight at the time and Mum wasn't well; I think Grandma had just died and Mum had her hands full with Rory. I remember I got told off for making such a fuss, but it took me a while to get to sleep at nights without him.

I place him carefully on my pillow and resolve to be more careful with him. He looks like an old-fashioned teddy bear, but he's not stiff and prickly, he's all squidgy and soft. He looks permanently worried, so at least we've got something in common.

I'm just about to go through my wardrobe, to see what horrors it holds, when I hear my dad come home.

My first thought is to run downstairs and fling my arms around him. I get as far as the top of the stairs before I realize that I'm nervous. It's strange having Mum and Dad in the same house. It's actually a bit overwhelming. I'm just telling myself not to be silly, and to get down there and make the most of it, when I hear them talking in the kitchen.

"I'd rather you didn't go out tonight," Mum's saying.

"There's no need to overreact, Susan. It's probably just a phase she's going through."

"Well, I'm worried about her. She asked me if you were coming home like she expected you not to. She must have heard us arguing—it can't be good for her to hear us like that . . ."

"If you stopped going on at me all the time there wouldn't be any arguing—"

"And if you stopped your gambling and drinking I wouldn't have to go on at you—"

This is not going well. I decide it's time I made an appearance, but as I approach the kitchen, I hear my mum say, "But if you'd heard her earlier—it was terrible, she was so rude to me . . ."

"Have you thought," replies my dad, "that it might be because you spoil her? Or maybe she's just not a very nice person and it's got nothing to do with us."

"Gary! How could you say such a thing about your own daughter? You know that's not true. She's a lovely child—normally."

I dash back upstairs, my cheeks burning. Did Dad really just say that about me? Maybe, I think, it's him that's not a very nice person.

I sit on the edge of my bed hugging Mr. Magoo. My mind goes back to last night and the argument I had with Imogen. It's not something I want to think about really, but maybe she's right. I have definitely got some anger issues with my mum. My fourteen-year-old self has always been angry that she left Dad and, come to that, I blamed Rory as well—but he's not even been born yet and they seem to be at each other's throats.

Of course, Mum and Dad's divorce wasn't the only reason I hated Mum. There was her illness as well, and how it made our lives so difficult. The only trouble is, I know now that you can't blame a person for being ill—it's not something they choose. If Mum had been ill with something else, something physical, I'd never have blamed her for that. It's just that depression is somehow harder to deal with. People are more sympathetic if you've got a physical illness. I suppose it's easier to understand.

At the moment, though, Mum hasn't left Dad and she hasn't got postnatal depression. She's still the old Mum—and I realize part of me was angry because she changed. But then I think back to how she is with Rory, when she gets the chance and she's not at work, that is. She's kind and loving to him and I wonder if she would still be with me if I'd let her. I feel a bit guilty sitting here—knowing what's in store for Mum while she's downstairs and doesn't have a clue. I jump when she calls me.

"Alice, tea's ready and Daddy's home."

It all sounds so normal. I have a picture of the real seven-year-old me running down the stairs and having tea with Mum and Dad—happy families.

As I enter the kitchen, my heart is racing, which is silly really, because it's only Mum and Dad. But it's still strange to see them in the same room, eating a meal together—being married.

"Hello, Princess," says Dad. "Mummy tells me you're feeling out of sorts." You could say that, I think—but it's a bit of an understatement.

"I'm fine now, thank you, Daddy," I tell him.

He smiles broadly and ruffles my hair. "That's my girl," he says. "Your mum tells me you've been behaving badly—but I told her my princess doesn't know how to be bad."

Like hell he did! I notice that he's sitting at the table reading the paper, the *Racing News* to be precise, while Mum is bustling around the kitchen, serving up the dinner and trying to feed Sooty at the same time because he's getting under her feet and meowing for his food. She's waddling because of her bump, which looks huge to me. I can't imagine having to put up with something that big stuck on the front of you. She looks tired. It should be her sitting there with her feet up, I think.

"I'll help you with that, Mummy. Why don't I feed Sooty?"

"Would you, love? Are you sure you can manage?" She looks reluctant and I know that she's thinking that if I help it'll just make more work—because she'll have to show me how to do it and probably clean up after I make a mess. Of course, what she doesn't know is that I've been feeding myself and Rory for years—so feeding a cat isn't exactly a problem for me.

"I'm sure I can manage," I tell her as I get a fork out of the cutlery draw. She smiles at me.

"I just know you're going to be such a help when this baby arrives," she says.

You have no idea, I think.

Tea, to be honest, is a bit of a strained affair. Mum asks me what I got up to at Sasha's and I have to make up a load of stuff about playing with her Barbie dolls, which I reckon is a fairly safe bet. "Playing with Sasha" is still a bit of an alien idea to me, but obviously it's nothing out of the ordinary for the seven-year-old me.

After tea Mum says, "You go and play for a bit, Alice, while I clear up, and then it'll be bath time."

I wander into the living room, where Dad is slumped in front of the television. As I approach him, he grabs hold of me and starts tickling. I'm laughing because I can't help it—he knows all my most ticklish spots—but I want him to stop, because it's embarrassing. Finally, I manage to wriggle away, and thankfully he doesn't get up off the sofa and chase me. I've got a feeling I used to enjoy that game. I can't think why. It makes me feel helpless, and small and weak, but I guess your average seven-year-old is used to feeling those things.

I watch the program with Dad for a bit; it's about giving someone's garden a makeover. Perhaps I ought to listen to it and get some tips on how to improve the garden at the George Street house. Then again, perhaps I should be thinking of ways to stop Mum and Dad getting divorced, and then I'll never even have to live in that horrible house.

"Daddy? Shall we go and help Mummy with the washing up?"

"Now, why would we want to do that, Princess?" he says.

"Well, she is very pregnant," I say, wondering why I have to state the obvious.

"Don't you worry your pretty head about that. Anyhow, she's finished now."

At that moment Mum calls down the stairs to me, "Alice, come upstairs."

I stop myself from yelling back, "Why? What do you want?" and go up.

When I reach the landing, Mum advances on me with a hairbrush in her hand. She unravels my braids and is about to start brushing.

"It's okay, Mum," I say, trying to take the brush from her, "I can do that myself."

She's about to argue, so I quickly add, "When Ror—I mean the baby . . . is born, you probably won't have time to do this sort of thing, so it would be better if I learn how to do it properly."

Reluctantly, she hands me the brush. "I expect you're right. But don't imagine that this baby is going to change things too much. I'll still have time for you, you know." She watches me brush my hair. "I can see you don't need my help with that any more, though. You're doing a grand job. I'll go and run your bath."

She disappears into the bathroom and I wonder how I can tell her that "this baby" is going to change our lives more than she can even begin to imagine.

A few minutes later she's back out again. "Right, get undressed." She stands there looking at me. Oh, my God, she's expecting me to get undressed in front of her! Then I think, what does it matter? Apart from the fact that this isn't really happening, what have I got to hide?

Still, as I undress and climb into the bath, I sort of wish Mum would go. She puts a box of toys on the bathroom stool. "You go ahead and play and I'll come and wash your hair in a bit," she tells me. I'm about to protest, but she's gone.

I ignore the bath toys and start to pick absently at the scab on my knee, but it's difficult to get a hold on. I inspect my nails. They're bitten down to the quick! Yuck, I don't remember being a nail-biter. Still, it shouldn't take too long to grow them back—they're tiny. Next, I look at my hair. It's so long the ends are trailing in the water. It's a lot more blonde than my fourteen-year-old hair, and finer as well.

I try to lie back in the bath, but I'm not long enough, and I slip down. Mum hasn't run it hot enough, but it's nice under the water with my ears submerged. I feel cut off from the world and strangely peaceful for the first time since this weird thing happened to me.

There are some foam letters stuck on the side of the bath and I play around with them, then realize I've spelled out the word, HELP. I'd better not let Mum see that; she'll start worrying again that something bad happened to me at Sasha's. It's a bit ironic really because "something bad" did happen at Sasha's; but that was last night and seven years in the future. God, I sound mad even to myself. To take my mind off it I start singing.

It sounds very odd because my ears are still under the water and it's easier to hit the high notes with my squeaky little voice. I imagine I sound quite cute.

I'm just getting into my underwater performance when Mum appears above me. I sit up quickly.

Mum's rubbing shampoo into my hair and rinsing it off by pouring water from an old red bucket that was in the toy box next to the bath. I'm about to complain and tell her it would be easier if I did it myself, in the shower, only I notice that there isn't a shower in here.

"We should get a shower," I tell Mum, although to be honest I'm quite enjoying having her wash my hair.

"Yes, well, there are a lot of things we should get," she says, holding out a towel. I stand up and she wraps the towel around me, giving me a hug at the same time.

"Dad's got a good job, though, hasn't he?" He's always telling me what a brilliant salesman he is.

"Daddy works on commission, which means that if he doesn't put in the work, he doesn't get the money. . . ." I get the distinct impression from the way she says this that Daddy does not put in the work.

Mum's finished drying me now and hands me my nightgown.

It's pink but, thankfully, devoid of Barbie. "Put your robe on and you can come downstairs for a bit, until your hair's dry," she says.

When I get into the living room, Dad's still sitting in front of the TV. He jumps up when Mum and I enter.

"Right, I'd better be off to the pub, then," he says. This is not good. How can we be a family if he's never here?

"Daddy?" I say in my cutest most wheedling voice. "Will you read me a story before you go?"

"I can't, my love. I'm already late as it is."

"Do you have to go? Why can't you stay here with me and Mummy?" I ask him, although, somehow, I can guess the answer.

"Because, my sweet, it's darts night and your old dad is on the team. You wouldn't want me to let the lads down, now, would you?"

"Oh no, you mustn't let the lads down." But what about your wife and daughter? I can't help wondering.

"That's my girl," he says, and disappears out of the door.

Mum offers to read me a story but, as it wasn't really a story I was after, I tell her that I'll be fine reading a book by myself. She comes upstairs and tucks me in. I've found an Agatha Christie in the bookcase in the living room and hidden it under my robe. When Mum passes me a copy of *Small Stories for Small Girls*, or something like that—I don't bother to look too closely—I thank her. When she's safely downstairs, I retrieve *Murder on the Orient Express*, cuddle up to Mr. Magoo, and try to get lost in some fiction.

It's funny, I think. If anyone ever wrote about what's happening to me, no one would ever believe it. In fact, I'm not sure that I believe it. Maybe when I wake up in the morning everything will be back to normal. Half of me is madly hoping that it will be, and the other half wants to stay here and sort things out. As I'm mulling over which one I'd prefer, I fall asleep.

* * *

I'm woken up by shouting coming from downstairs. I immediately put my head under the pillow and nearly poke my eye out with the pencil I left there. Damn, that means my life hasn't gone back to normal while I was asleep, and I'm still in the Barbie bed.

The seven-year-old Alice might have hidden her head under the pillow, but there are no such luxuries for me. I need to know what's going on so I can fix it. I open my bedroom door carefully and creep along the landing until I'm at the top of the stairs. Mum and Dad are in the kitchen, but the door is open, so I can easily hear them. They're not making any attempt to keep their voices down; Dad because he's drunk and Mum because she's too angry.

". . . and what's going to happen when the baby's born and I *can't* work?" That's Mum obviously.

"You should have thought about that before you got yourself pregnant!"

"I didn't *get myself pregnant*! That was you, remember? I told you it wasn't safe, but you were too bloody drunk to listen, so don't blame that on me!"

I don't know why they're trying to blame each other for the baby. Everyone knows it takes two to get pregnant, for heaven's sake. And that's Rory they're talking about. I almost feel sorry for him—it's not exactly his fault, I think indignantly. I realize that I'm biting my nails.

Dad's making his way down the hall, so I dash back to bed. My insides feel all quivery and jumpy and knotted, all at the same time, which is not a pleasant feeling. I hear the door creak open and the landing light makes my room brighter. I can tell this even though I've got my eyes tight shut. I breathe slowly, pretending to be asleep. Someone bends over my bed and kisses me and I can tell, from the soapy smell and tickle of her hair, that it's Mum. The sleep thing has obviously fooled her but then, before she can move away, I grab her hand.

"Oh, Alice! You gave me a shock. I thought you were asleep."

I'm about to point out that as she didn't provide me with

earplugs at bedtime that isn't very likely, but decide against it. She's probably had enough for one night without having to deal with a precocious daughter.

"The shouting woke me up," I tell her. I'm not going to let her off the hook altogether.

"I'm sorry, darling," she says. "Try not to let it bother you."

Not bother me? Is she mad?

"Daddy and I still love you, you know, even though we don't always see eye to eye." Oh, please! Not that old chestnut! But then I remember that Mum thinks I'm seven, so perhaps it's all right.

"Now, get some sleep, you've got school tomorrow." She bends down and kisses me again. "And don't worry, it'll all be fine," she tells me and leaves before I can put her right on that one.

Now I'm doubly worried. School! Aaarrgh!

Chapter Four

When I wake up in the morning, I'm really tired and it's a huge effort to get out of bed. I'm a bit disappointed. Rory always bounces out of bed way too early and runs around like a lunatic. I had sort of assumed that, as a seven-year-old, I, too, would be full of energy. Then I remember that I hardly got any sleep last night, so it's not exactly surprising that I feel like this. Mum's been in and left my clothes out ready for me to put on. That's a bit weird—like having a personal maid. Still, I'm not complaining. I go into the bathroom, wash my hands and face, and clean my teeth.

Normally, about now, on a school day, I'd be panicking. Am I having a bad-hair day? Have I got too much makeup on? Will I be made to go and wash it off during homeroom? Or have I not put enough on? Do I look like one of the geeks? Have I done all my homework? How horrid is Sasha going to be today?

Instead, I brush my hair out and try and decide what to do with it. I'm tempted to do one French braid down the back, but realize that it might take some explaining to Mum, because I'm sure I couldn't do that when I was seven.

In fact, I doubt I did anything for myself at that age, the way Mum is running around after me. That might go some way to explaining why life was so hard after Rory arrived. Mum suddenly stopped doing *anything* and even had trouble getting out of bed some mornings. I wasn't very well prepared for looking after myself.

I put on the long white socks, skirt, white shirt, and red sweatshirt. It's got Cromwell Primary School embroidered around the school shield, which has an owl in the middle. I remember I always loved that owl.

I make my way downstairs and realize my stomach is knotted again, but I think it might be because I'm excited as well as nervous. It feels like my first day at school, but the problem is—it isn't. For Mum, and everyone at school, this will just be a normal day. For me, on the other hand, it's going to be a very strange experience.

I pass the living room on my way to the kitchen and notice there's a load of bedding folded up on the sofa. If Dad slept in there last night things must be bad. I really need to give some thought as to what I'm going to do about the Mum-Dad situation. I'll have a proper think after I've got this school thing out of the way. At least I won't have heaps of homework tonight.

"You're very quiet," says Mum on the way to school. We're walking there, but not very fast, because of Mum's waddle. I'm thinking about what lies ahead for me. I went through my schoolbag after breakfast. It would appear that we're doing Ancient Egypt, Our Town—Past and Present, and we've got spelling today. I'm in Year Three, which means my teacher is Miss Carter. I liked her. She was fun and kind.

But it's not the work and the teachers that are worrying me, I finally admit to myself. It's the other children and how I'm going to behave around them. Okay, it's not even the idea of "other children" that's making my stomach turn somersaults. Let's face it—it's Sasha. I feel like a condemned prisoner being led to the gallows. If Sasha at fourteen is a bitch and a bully, what's she going to be like at seven? Not only that, if I'm her friend, I'll probably have to sit next to her all day.

Mum takes my hand as we cross the main road and, when we get to the other side, I don't let go. She doesn't seem to find this odd, but as we approach the school gates, my grip tightens.

"What's the matter, darling?" Mum asks, picking up on my anxiety.

And because I can't say, "I'm terrified, can we go back home, please?" I make do with, "Nothing—I'm fine."

Just as I'm contemplating pulling a sicky, right here, right now—I'm sure I can convince Mum I'm ill after yesterday—she's waving me off, saying, "I'll see you at three, love," and she's gone!

I hover at the gate, watching all the children madly tearing around the playground. Come on, Alice, I tell myself. For heaven's sake! They're only a bunch of kids!

Someone's tugging at my sleeve. "Did you bring it?" I turn round and there's Sasha. God, she looks hilarious, all little and puny—but still a bit scary. Her hair is pulled back into a high ponytail and she's jumping up and down. She's only seven, I tell myself. How bad can it be?

"Why are you staring at me like that? Did you bring it? Give it to me, quick."

"Bring what?" I ask cautiously.

"The skipping rope, stupid. Like I told you. How are we going to play the game without a skipping rope?" she asks, stamping her foot.

I wish I knew what she was talking about. I haven't skipped for years. I look around the playground at the other children. I recognize some of them from my school—the secondary school, that is. They do look funny, sort of like themselves but not. I spot Luke O'Connor playing tag—he looks quite cute. And there's Chelsea Fuller and Clara White, Sasha's cronies. They've both got skipping ropes.

"Why don't we go and play with Clara and Chelsea?" I say to Sasha. Not that I want to—at all—but it might get her off my back for a bit.

"What? Don't be silly, we hate them." We do? Oh. Okay. "That's why you were meant to bring the skipping rope today, so we can play the game before they do." This, obviously, is making no sense to me.

"And this is important—because . . . ?" I say.

"Because," says Sasha, seriously exasperated now, "otherwise, everyone will think we're copying them, when really it's them that'll be copying us."

Oh yes, of course. As if I haven't got anything better to think about.

"Have you seen Imogen?" I ask desperately. If ever I needed a friend it's now, and thankfully she'll still be talking to me because we haven't argued yet.

"Who?"

"Im–o–gen," I say slowly and clearly.

"Never heard of her," says Sasha. "I can't believe you forgot the skipping rope. I thought you were my friend."

Luckily, the bell rings at this moment so I don't have to tell her that actually, I'd rather hang from a rope by my hair than hang around with her.

As everyone runs to line up in their class groups, I get the chance to worry about why Imogen isn't here, and why Sasha hasn't even heard of her. *She* was my best friend at primary school, not Sasha.

Then I remember—she didn't come to this school from the beginning. They moved here from London and Imogen became my friend—when? If only I could remember when.

We file into the cloakroom and hang our coats up. I decide to try and keep a low profile until I've got used to being back here. If I just follow what everyone else does it shouldn't be too difficult.

When I walk into class 3C I feel all nostalgic. There's stuff stuck up all over the walls, things we've painted and written. There's a huge blue and gold sarcophagus that we've painted; obviously part of the Ancient Egypt project. I remember that from before, because it scared me all the time it was up on the wall. I look at it now and wonder why. Okay, the eyes are a bit spooky, but I can't have been that much of a wimp at seven, could I?

There's a nature table in the corner covered with leaves and pinecones and a bird's nest. Behind Miss Carter's desk there's even a blackboard. By the time I reached Year Six these had all been replaced by white boards and laptops. I'm just wondering what hasn't been invented yet—like iPhones and maybe even MP3 players—when Miss Carter comes in. I'm so happy to see her again that I nearly run up and hug her. Not really a cool thing to do.

"Settle down, children," she says, and everyone rushes to their seats. I hang back a bit until I can see which chair is left, and, of course, it's the one next to Sasha.

"Wake up, Alice," calls Miss Carter. "We've got a lot to get through today."

We start with a spelling test, which is painfully slow but not what you'd call demanding, as the hardest word is *thought*. Still, I'm unaccountably pleased when I get 20 out of 20 and Sasha only gets 17.

"*Very* good, Alice. Well done, come and get a sticker," says Miss Carter, and I go up and she sticks a smiley sun onto my red sweatshirt. When I get back to my seat, Sasha pinches me on the top of my arm.

"Ow! What was that for?" I say.

"Smarty pants," is her only reply. I get the feeling Sasha doesn't like being outsmarted, but since she's not particularly bright, I decide that she's just going to have to get used to it.

It's fun getting everything right. Whenever Miss Carter asks a question, both Sasha and I put our hands up. She shoots hers up and stretches it as far as it will go, ramrod straight, whereas mine sort of flops around in the air, halfway up. I soon discover that Sasha is in the habit of putting her hand up whether she knows the answer or not. She might as well stick a sign on it saying, *Over here! Me! Me! Please notice me*. It's pathetic really, and after she gets a couple of answers wrong—and I get them right—she's in a very bad mood indeed.

This isn't improved at playtime when the rest of the girls start playing the game that Sasha was so desperate to start. It turns out to be called Ponies and consists of one girl being the pony and holding the rope round her waist while the other stands behind, holding each end of the "reins." The pony then trots around the playground neighing, while the other one—the rider—runs behind.

We're sitting on the playing field, in the shade of a big oak tree. Sasha is still blaming me for forgetting the skipping rope. As you can imagine, I am hugely relieved that we don't have one, or I would be running around neighing and feeling like a right idiot.

"Let's play Puppies instead," says Sasha.

I don't want to know what this entails, but she's telling me, anyway.

"I'll be the little girl, you're the puppy, and I come into the pet shop and buy you and then I take you to the vet—I'll have to be the vet as well but that's okay—and then I take you home and teach you loads of tricks."

Even Sasha has to take a breath occasionally, so I butt in. "I don't feel like playing Puppies. Let's just sit here and do *nothing*." This is definitely the wrong thing to say. Sasha puts her hands on her hips.

"What is wrong with you today? We can't do nothing. Look, you be the puppy. . . ."

It occurs to me that the seven-year-old Alice was a bit shy and timid and probably fell in with whatever Sasha told her to do. Mind you, she is extremely bossy.

But sitting under the tree I look at her and realize that she's just a kid, not much older than Rory, and I've had a lot of experience handling him. This girl has made my life hell for the past seven years, and I suddenly wonder why I let it happen. Why did I let her take control of my feelings and trample all over them?

She might have found the seven-year-old Alice a walkover, but not this one. I'll play with her if she wants. I've just thought of a brand new game. It's called Cat and Mouse and I am going to be the cat. I'm going to toy with Sasha and then I'm going to chew her up and spit her out.

"Sasha?" I say in my sweetest voice. "Did anyone ever tell you that you have a bit of a problem?"

"What kind of puppy do you want to be? A Labrador or a spaniel?"

"Listen, I'm telling you this because I'm your friend, okay?" I say in a sympathetic tone, placing my hand on her arm. Now I've got her attention.

"Telling me what?"

"About your problem. You know, why no one else will play with you. Don't get cross with me for telling you, I just think you should know."

Sasha looks confused and, I'm glad to see, also slightly worried. "What do you mean, no one else will play with me? What problem?"

I look her in the eye. "Sasha, the thing is—your breath really smells."

Goal! She looks mortified, but this is Sasha we're talking about, and the mortification lasts only a second before it's replaced by defiance.

"It does not!"

As she says this, I pull away slightly and wrinkle my nose.

"You're a liar, Alice Watkins, and I'm not playing with you anymore," and she runs off. I watch her go. This isn't going to be easy, but I know I can do it. It requires subtlety, which is something that Sasha doesn't understand. Mind you, I must have made some headway, because rather than going to join the other girls in the playground, Sasha has run into the cloakroom, no doubt to check on her "bad breath."

I make my way around the playground telling everyone that Sasha has an illness, and that it is very contagious, and they'd be advised to keep their distance and not let her breathe on them. Otherwise, they too will get *Bratalgia*, which stunts your growth and makes you extremely fat in later life.

I soon discover that my former timidity and shyness is paying off. Everyone believes me—it seems that the younger Alice was not a girl to tell lies or be nasty. Yippee! My job just got a whole lot easier.

When Sasha comes out of the cloakroom she gives me an evil look and runs off to play with Chelsea and Clara. As she talks to them, they back off slightly and Clara even puts her hand over her nose. I can see that they're explaining to her that Ponies is a two-person game and then they trot off across the playing field. Sasha looks around and in her desperation picks on Lauren Hall and Mary Butler. She couldn't have made a worse choice. Mary, I happen to know, is the vainest girl ever born. When she's fourteen, she will spend all her lunchtimes in the bathroom putting on makeup. So, when Sasha approaches them, Mary lets out a little squeal, grabs Lauren by the hand, and runs off. The thought of catching a disease that will make her fat drives Mary to the furthest corner of the playing field.

Sasha comes back to me. "Look, I'm sorry I just called you a liar. I think you must be right." She looks really upset.

Bearing in mind the saying, "Keep your friends close and your enemies closer," I say, "That's okay. How about that game of Puppies, then?"

Mercifully, the bell goes before she gets a chance to pat me on the head and buy me off the imaginary shopkeeper.

As we're standing in line to go in, I surreptitiously kick the boy standing in front of Sasha. Luckily for me it's Jake Hudson, the biggest and meanest boy in the school. When I say big, I mean in every way. He's big boned, bigheaded, and bigmouthed. When he turns around I'm innocently talking to the girl behind me, and he thinks his attacker is Sasha. He pushes her so she stumbles into me and I fall back onto the girl behind who treads on the girl behind her. A chorus of protest goes up along the line and mutterings of, "It wasn't me, it was Sasha," can be heard.

"Watch it, Stinky!" says Jake to Sasha. If I remember right, Jake calls everyone Stinky, but Sasha has obviously forgotten this piece of information and as we file into the classroom, I see her breathing into her hand, trying to smell her breath.

Sasha is uncharacteristically quiet all afternoon, which leaves me to get on with writing a brilliant story in literacy. Miss Carter is very impressed and gets me to read it out in front of everyone. I know that if I'd had to do that when I was seven I would have died of embarrassment. Now, although I'm a bit nervous because everyone is staring at me, I just imagine that I'm reading a story to Rory. Afterward I get another sticker and when Miss Carter is putting it on my sweater, next to the other one, she says, "This really is an amazing piece of work. If you hadn't done it in class I would have thought you'd had some help with it."

I decide it might be a good idea to tone down my "brilliance" a bit. I don't want to cause a stir or get noticed too much. I've got too many other things to think about without being labeled a child genius—tempting though it is. Mind you, Miss Carter's next words burst my bubble a bit.

"Watch your handwriting, though, Alice, it's getting a little bit messy." I'll have to work on making it more rounded and childish.

When I get back to my desk, I'm expecting another pinch from Sasha, but to my surprise she smiles at me and says, "That was a really good story." She looks almost proud to be my friend—which is a deeply weird experience.

"You look happy," says Mum when she picks me up. "Did you make it up with Sasha?"

"Oh yes, me and Sasha are fine now," I tell her as I skip along beside her. My good mood stays with me all afternoon, and I help Mum make the tea and then we play a game of ludo. It's not until seven o'clock, when Mum's telling me it's bedtime, that I realize Dad hasn't come home. I was too busy thinking about Rory's absence to notice Dad hadn't showed up. I'm so used to him not being around that I forgot he should be here, with us.

"Daddy has to work late tonight," Mum tells me as we pack the game away. She doesn't sound too happy about it and she looks tired, so I decide not to kick up a fuss about having to go to bed so early. Besides, I'm exhausted after my day at school. Then I remember that she's been at work all day. "How was Miss Maybrooke?" I ask her.

"Fancy you remembering that. She's a lovely lady, we got along really well and she made me sit and drink tea most of the time. She said a woman in my condition shouldn't be working, but I explained to her that I didn't have a lot of choice. I tidied her kitchen up a bit, though. She lives in a lovely house, really unspoiled—well, apart from the bathroom that is. It's nearly all original."

Mum's perched on the side of the bath, watching me to make sure I brush my teeth properly, but I don't mind. It's nice talking to her, like this.

When Mum's tucked me in and kissed me, she goes downstairs and I get my notebook out. I open it and review my list:

1. Stop Sooty from getting run over.

Short of keeping him locked in a cupboard for the rest of his life, I'm not sure how I'm going to manage this. Perhaps I could give him some road safety lessons. Or some traffic aversion therapy. That might work. I'll have to give it some more thought.

2. Stop Mum and Dad from splitting up.

This last one is obviously the biggy.

3. Find a way to get back to reality.

I add a question mark after this one. I can't go back yet—there's too much to do. I add:

4. Make Sasha's life hell.

That should be easy; I've got it well in hand. I need to concentrate on number two. Perhaps I could get hold of some marriage guidance leaflets and place them strategically around the house.

Then I have an idea. Maybe I can stop them getting divorced by behaving really badly. I remember when I was in Year Eight, there was a girl in my class who refused to get out of bed when her parents split up. She was off school for ages, but then she moved away with her mum, who went back north after the divorce. That obviously didn't work, then.

Or there was that girl in Year Nine. She was very quiet and shy until her parents got divorced, then she went right off the rails. She shaved off all her hair and started fooling around with loads of boys, and there were rumors that she was self harming.

She left eventually, as well. Anyhow, her radical behavior didn't stop her parents from getting divorced either.

In fact, just thinking about that girl has made me so depressed I feel like giving the whole thing up. I'm about to put my notebook away when I hear my dad come back. He's in a good mood and I can hear Mum laughing at something he's said. It's like being a proper family again and I don't want it to stop.

Right, I just need to look at this in a different way. I have the advantage here because I'm seeing it in retrospect. I need to persuade Mum that our life will be awful if she leaves Dad. I need to show her that she needs him. I decide to write down everything I know about the divorce, so I turn to the back of the notebook and make a fresh start.

I know that Mum threw Dad out, because Dad told me all about it. Dad often has a moan about Mum, so I do know that she stopped loving him and made him move out, and he was heartbroken to leave us behind. He had nowhere to go and ended up camping out on the floor of a flat belonging to a workmate. The workmate just happened to be Trish and, according to Dad, she was very kind and sweet so that he ended up falling in love with her, and they've been together ever since. Even though she's quite a bit younger than him.

It wasn't long after Rory was born that all this happened, so I'd better get a move on. Why did Mum throw him out? I chew the end of my pencil while I give this some thought.

It doesn't help that Mum never says anything against Dad. She has a strict policy of not criticizing Dad in front of me and Rory because, she says, however she feels about him, he's still our dad. That's all very well, but it means that I don't know how she feels about him. If she'd ranted and raved I might have a clearer idea as to why she did it.

How can I explain to Mum that if she throws Dad out she will be forcing him into the arms of another woman? Surely that would make her jealous and she might see sense. Unfortunately, I don't know how I'd manage that without her thinking I've turned into some freaky psychic overnight, assuming, of course, she believes me—which she won't.

How I can stop Mum falling out of love with Dad? I suck the end of my braid and stare into space, trying to think of an idea. I'm disturbed by raised voices coming from downstairs. Oh no, not again! They were laughing a minute ago. I creep out onto the landing to find out what it's about this time and hear Mum's shrill voice.

"All I'm asking is that you stop spending so much money down the pub and at the bookies. You promised you'd stop the gambling when I got pregnant, so what's this . . .?"

I can see through the banisters that she's waving a betting slip in his face.

"And you promised you'd stop nagging me . . ."

He's got a point. At this rate she won't have to throw him out—she'll drive him away.

"If you won't do it for me, then do it for your children. You've got a family to look after . . ."

"I never wanted the bloody children in the first place. It's hardly surprising that I spend all my time down at the pub when all I get here is a whiny daughter and a nagging wife."

He slams out of the front door and I crawl back into bed and pull the covers over my head. I can hear Mum crying in the living room.

I don't whine, do I?

Chapter Five

The next morning, I spring out of bed with all the energy of a hyperactive seven-year-old. At least that's what it feels like. My good mood is slightly marred, though, when I walk into the kitchen and see Dad sitting at the table finishing his toast and marmalade. I find it difficult to look him in the eye when I remember what he said about me last night.

"And how's my little Princess, this morning?" he asks in a bright voice, which sounds forced, now I know his true feelings.

"Oh, just my usual, whiny self," I say sweetly, as I sit down. I really can't help myself.

I notice him exchanging a look with Mum over my head. "I'd better be off, then," he says, pushing back his chair and standing up. An avalanche of toast crumbs fall to the floor. I can hear them crunching underfoot as he goes over to Mum and gives her a kiss. "Someone has to keep this family in the style to which it's become accustomed." He laughs.

If that's a joke it's not a very good one, in the present circumstances. Mum laughs, because she always laughs at Dad's jokes, but I don't think she sounds very amused.

Dad slips out of the door and Mum gets the dustpan and brush from the closet. She tries to sweep up the toast crumbs but the bump prevents her from bending down. I take the dustpan and brush from her and clean up the mess. I wonder why Mum wants another baby when she's already looking after the biggest one in the world—namely, Dad.

"What was it that made you fall in love with Dad?" I ask. I'm attempting to get Mum to remember how she used to feel about him, in the hope that she'll see what a great bloke he is.

The problem is it comes out all wrong, so it sounds like I'm saying, "What the hell did you ever see in him?" Although, actually, I *am* beginning to wonder. I'm not entirely sure Dad is such a great bloke, after all.

"Your father," says mum, "can be a very charming man when he wants to be." She's got a faraway look in her eyes and a stupid grin on her face, and she's rubbing her hands over her bump. Oh, my God! She's thinking about sex! Yuck! And they were only arguing about that the other night! What is it with adults? I wish they'd make up their minds. One minute they're shouting each other's heads off, and the next minute they're all lovey-dovey.

"He's under an awful lot of pressure at the moment, though," says Mum, "at work and with the new baby on the way. He does have his little failings, I admit, but I love him all the same."

I stare at Mum. I've got my mouth open again. The gambling and drinking are hardly "little failings." She's not even lying to me about loving Dad. She really means it, I can tell. I'm confused.

"So how come he slept on the sofa last night?" I ask.

Mum laughs. "Because I threw him out of the bed. I'm so big at the moment there isn't really room for him as well and neither of us were getting any sleep, so he went downstairs instead."

It seems that not everything is as it appears. But that doesn't answer the question. If Mum is still so "in love" with Dad, why is she about to leave him?

I try to persuade Mum that I'm perfectly capable of walking to school on my own, but she won't hear of it.

"Maybe when you're a bit older, Alice." God, and there was me thinking that I didn't have any freedom at fourteen! At least I wasn't escorted everywhere like a prisoner.

I go up to my room to get my school things ready. If Mum does still love Dad, then her reason for leaving him must have been the gambling and drinking. If I can get him to stop, then maybe we can all live happily ever after. The problem is, I get the feeling it would be easier to persuade the pope to convert to Buddhism than to get my dad to change his ways.

I've got some serious research to do. I need to find out about support groups for Dad, like Alcoholics Anonymous. And there must be a similar thing for people with a gambling problem. Gamblers Anonymous maybe. And I might as well find out everything I can about postnatal depression while I'm at it. If we had a computer this would be easy. It's not the sort of thing that I'm going to find in the school library, I really need to get to the public library. An idea forms itself in my head.

As we make our slow, waddly way to school, I say to Mum, "Don't forget I'm going to Sasha's for tea tonight."

Mum has stopped to catch her breath. She's breathing quite heavily and luckily not paying too much attention to me, which makes a nice change.

"What? Are you sure? I don't remember that."

"Yes, it's all arranged," I lie cheerfully. "I'm going home with Sasha after school and her mum will bring me home."

"Okay, that's quite a relief actually. I'm feeling a bit sluggish today."

"I'll see you later, then," and I give her a kiss and run into the playground. Now, after school, I can nip off to the library and when I get home I'll pretend I've been to Sasha's and Mum will never be any the wiser.

It's quite a relief to be at school. At least now all I have to worry about is being horrible to Sasha. Easy-peasy, lemon squeezy.

It's still weird to see all these people I know as little kids again. It strikes me that they're not really all that much different to their fourteen-year-old selves. Lauren Hall, who I sit with in math, is painfully shy; I can see her clinging to her mum at the school gates. Lucy Clark is surrounded by a load of friends, girls as well as boys; Luke is fooling around with them in his cheerful, funny way; and Chelsea and Clara have separated themselves from the crowd and are leaning against the wall, whispering together and looking superior. It's just me that's different. My seven-year-old self would have been playing happily with Sasha, no doubt, trying to stay out of trouble and thinking about not very much except Barbie, probably. Oh, the blissful ignorance I lived in!

Someone's tugging at my sleeve. "Did you bring the skipping rope?"

"No," I tell her, and then before she can yell at me I say, "Ponies is a stupid game, anyway." She's about to argue so I add, "It's a bit babyish running around pretending to be a horse."

I can tell Sasha is dying to play at being a horse, but I also know that she won't want to be thought of as babyish. Nothing is going to get me to play one of those "pretending games," though. I know I used to love them, but I'm way too old to play them now.

Sasha is looking cross and puzzled. She's probably wondering what has happened to the pliable, meek, and easily bossed around little playmate that I used to be.

"Well, you thought the game up in the first place—so it's *you* that's babyish." She puts her hands on her hips and sticks her bottom lip out. I can't help laughing at her as she flounces off.

The bell goes, and as we line up, I find myself thinking about Imogen again and wishing she was here.

I decide during assembly that Sasha hasn't suffered enough yet. I need to up the ante. I think it's time we gave her the silent treatment.

I put my plan into action at playtime. When everyone rushes outside, I hang back and go up to Miss Carter at her desk. I arrange my face into its best "little girl lost" look and even wring my hands in despair.

"What is it, Alice?" she asks kindly. I have a moment of regret for lying to her in this way, but remind myself that it's not really a lie, I'm just complaining about something before it actually happens.

"The thing is . . ." I gulp.

"Yes?" This is really going to have to be good, because Miss

Carter is not stupid and she must know that little girls fight all the time. I decide to go in with the heavy guns.

"Mummy would have come to see you herself, only she's not well, with the baby on the way and everything. I wouldn't have bothered her with it normally because she's got enough on her plate with Daddy's gambling and drinking"—Miss Carter is really listening now. I'd better be careful or she'll have social services down on us—"but she noticed, what with the nightmares and me wetting the bed suddenly." Miss Carter's eyes look as if they're about to pop out.

"Why? Whatever's the matter?" she says.

"It's Sasha," I whisper, finally letting the tears fall.

"What about Sasha?" says Miss Carter. I can tell from her tone of voice that she knows full well just what Sasha is capable of.

"She really scares me," I say, looking really frightened. "She said if I told, she'd come and kill the baby when it's born."

Now I really do feel scared because I can't believe I'm actually doing this. Have I gone too far? Surely even Sasha wouldn't be that horrible. Miss Carter seems to have no trouble believing it, though, which gives me the strength to carry on.

"She won't let me be friends with anyone else, and when you're not looking"—I pause, dramatically—"she hurts me."

I remind myself that Sasha did actually pinch me the other day after the spelling test, so it's not a complete fib.

"The thing is . . . Mummy was hoping that you could move me to a different desk, but please, please, please can you do it so that Sasha doesn't know I've said anything. And please don't say anything to her about the bullying."

Miss Carter looks very worried and not totally convinced about the "not saying anything" clause. I mean, these are quite serious offenses—threats to kill and grievous bodily harm usually carry a prison sentence—but we are only seven, I can see her thinking, and that it will probably all blow over soon.

She pats me kindly on the shoulder. "Don't worry about it anymore. I've had a great idea, but I can't do anything about it right now, so I need you to be a brave girl for a little bit longer." She hands me a tissue and I mop up my crocodile tears.

"Thank you, Miss Carter," I say, and dash out into the playground. At least I won't have to sit next to Sasha for much longer.

I've got a lot of work to do before playtime is over. I start with Chelsea and Clara. Going over to them I say, "Can I play with you?"

They stop what they're doing and stare at me, but don't tell me to push off, so I carry on. "It's just that Sasha's not talking to me. Well, actually, the truth is—I'm not talking to her."

They both look interested now, so I get truly stuck in.

"She said you're stupid and smelly and ugly and she's going to invite everyone to her party except you two. I didn't think that was very fair, and I told her you were nice, so then she picked on me and said I was stupid and smelly, too, so I decided I wasn't going to talk to her anymore."

Chelsea and Clara fall for it. "Well, you can play with us and we won't talk to her either."

We're just beginning a game of tag, which I've initiated so that I can run around the playground and stir up more trouble with the other kids in our class, when Sasha comes up.

"Come on, Alice. Why are you playing with these copycats? I thought we were playing Puppies." I turn my back on her and look scared.

This seems to give Chelsea courage. "Go away—you're stupid and ugly and smelly." Chelsea grabs me and Clara and we all run off. Sasha looks surprised at this outburst, but I can tell that the *smelly* hasn't been lost on her.

By the end of the lunch break, Sasha is well and truly out in the cold. No one is talking to her, and it doesn't stop there. It seems that I've set something in motion for which Sasha only has herself to blame. She's been bossy and horrid to everyone at some point, but so far no one's actually stood up to her. As all the children in our class realize that everyone is in on it, the campaign takes on a life of its own, and I just sit back and watch.

Sasha doesn't really realize I'm not talking to her at first because the morning is spent doing a times table test and then personal reading time. But at lunchtime I run off with Chelsea and Clara. Sasha tries to join in with the others, but every single one of them turns their back on her and eventually she plays with some of the little children from Year One. I can see her bossing them about as I skip around the playground with Clara's skipping rope. She keeps looking my way with a puzzled look on her face, but I just look straight through her as if she's not there.

After lunch we have to get changed for PE, which is taught by our headmistress, Miss Strickland. I remember that I was absolutely terrified of her and kept out of her way as much as possible.

She takes us outside and tells us to get into pairs. Sasha is immediately at my side. Personally, I was hoping to pair up with Lucy Clark. I've always liked Lucy, and she's the one I was watching from the art-room window, in my old life, and wishing that I was in her group of friends because they always seem to have so much fun. She's paired up with Miranda Wilkes, though, and as everyone else is now in pairs it looks like I'm stuck with Sasha.

Miss Strickland is handing out tennis balls and telling us to practice our throwing and catching. Sasha and I stand opposite each other, throwing the ball back and forth. It isn't long before I get seriously bored by this. To be fair, Sasha isn't bad at it. She doesn't drop the ball as often as some of the kids, judging by the numbers that are running around chasing balls all over the playground. I can tell I'm the best by a long shot. I'm waiting for Miss Strickland to notice, and praise me for my skill, only she doesn't, because she's not even watching us. She's talking to the caretaker about the drainpipes.

"Come on!" says Sasha, impatiently. "Throw me the ball."

"Okay," I tell her. "Catch this, Bossy Boots," and I lob the ball as hard as I can, right over her head. There's a moment when I think it might hit the window and break it, but thankfully I've thrown it too high, and it bounces off the roof. I'm about to let out a sigh of relief when one of the tiles slides gently down the roof. It lands with a smash on the tarmac between Miss Strickland and the caretaker. One of the shards of tile hits the headmistress on the leg, cutting her shin and causing her tights to run.

At the sound of the smashing tile, all the children stop what they're doing and a deafening hush descends on the playground. Not for long, though.

Miss Strickland shouts, "Which stupid child threw that ball?" I go hot and then cold and I'm about to step forward, on very shaky legs, when Sasha's hand shoots up into the air next to me, nearly taking my ear off.

"I did, Miss Strickland," says Sasha. Her cheeks are slightly pink, but her chin is held high. I try to catch her eye. Surely this isn't another of her bids for attention? Did her hand go up automatically like it does in class? But she won't look at me. Sasha and Miss Strickland's eyes are locked.

"My office. Now, young lady. The rest of you go and get changed—quietly!"

As I put my uniform back on I wonder what's happening in the headmistress's office. I wonder, if it was me in there now and not Sasha, if I would have the nerve to tell Miss Strickland that she should have been paying attention to the class, and that it was an accident, and she shouldn't punish small children for accidents. Somehow, I doubt it. She still terrifies me.

We file back into the classroom and the other children tell Miss Carter what happened. I feel really bad. No one, except Sasha, saw me throw that ball.

When she comes back in, all the other children stare at her and giggle, but she holds her head high and takes her seat next to me. Reluctantly, I have to admire her style.

"What did you do that for?" I whisper as we all make our way to the carpet area where Miss Carter is getting ready to read to us before hometime.

"It's okay," says Sasha. "I know how scared you are of Miss Strickland. She was horrible and she would *definitely* have made you cry, but all the time she was shouting at me I just pictured her sitting on the toilet with her underwear around her knees." Sasha laughs and squeezes my hand. "I pretended she was constipated because she was so red in the face."

I laugh, too, at this image of horrible Miss Strickland. "I can't believe you'd do that for me," I tell Sasha. And it's true, I can't.

"Of course I would, silly. You're my best friend."

At home time, when we're in the cloakroom getting our coats on, the other girls are still being mean to Sasha. Because nobody's talking to her, this generally consists of bumping into her and whispering about her while giving her sly looks. I now feel really bad about what's happening.

I try to remind myself how horrible Sasha has been to me all through secondary school. This is a very odd feeling because we're all seven and secondary school is miles off for us, but the truth is it happened—and I must remember that.

The trouble is, though, aren't I being just as bad? What if I turn into the Bitch Queen from hell? I try to console myself with the thought that I'm simply getting my own back on Sasha for the way she's treated me. But she hasn't actually treated me like that yet, which makes me feel doubly mean because she doesn't know why it's happening.

The trouble is, it did feel great to begin with, but now I'm not so sure. I feel kind of depressed about it. Like I'm some big kid picking on a small kid. I know we appear to be the same age, but deep down I'm still fourteen and ought to know better.

Still, enough of this. I need to go to the library now and put my "Save the Watkins family" campaign into action.

Outside in the playground I walk as nonchalantly as possible toward the gates so that nobody realizes I'm leaving on my own. I'm just about to slip out when I hear my name being called.

There's a woman standing at the gates waiting for me, and it isn't my mother. Oh, my God! It's my gran!

Chapter Six

"Hello, hunnybun," says Gran. "I bet you weren't expecting to see me."

She's not wrong there. I'm so overcome, I'm speechless. Of all the weird situations that this weird situation I'm in has thrown up, this has to be the weirdest yet. In fact, it's a bit scary. Seeing someone who is by all accounts dead is not something I'm used to. Okay, so it happened with Miss Maybrooke and even Sooty, but this is different. This is my own gran!

Of course, there's nothing unusual about it for Gran. She's carrying on like nothing is weird.

"Your mum had to go into the hospital this morning, so I've come to look after you. Isn't that exciting? A new baby sister—or brother—on the way."

I force my mouth into a smile.

She carries on. "I hope you don't mind not going to Sasha's for tea tonight. I suppose I'd better have a word with her mum and explain what's happening."

This galvanizes me out of my stupor. "It's okay, Gran. I'll sort it out," and I dash off across the playground to where Sasha is standing while her mum chats away to some of the other mums. Obviously, I've got to say something now I'm here and it can't be, "Sorry, I can't come to tea after all," so when Sasha smiles at me and says, "Hello," I say, "Look, I'm really sorry about earlier—you know—playing with Clara and Chelsea and everything. And thank you for what you did. About the ball and stuff. It was really nice of you." And I realize, as I'm saying it, that I actually am sorry.

"Shall I ask my mum if you can come to tea tonight?" she says. "We could play that Puppy game."

"I can't, not today—my gran's here. I think my mum's having the baby. Maybe another night."

Walking home with Gran is really difficult. I want to tell her about all the things that have happened since she died, about how Mum and Dad divorced and about moving to George Street, about school and having to help with Rory, and maybe even about Seth. I'm bursting with all this information and I can't tell her any of it because it hasn't happened yet. Because I'm so busy not saying all this I end up saying nothing.

"You're very quiet today," comments Gran. "I hope you're not worrying about your mum. She'll be fine. We'll call the hospital when we get home and see how she's doing."

Actually, I am worried. I haven't really thought too much about Mum giving birth. I've been too wrapped up in adjusting to my new life with Mum and Dad and haven't really realized it was going to happen so soon. I'm terrified that I'm running out of time and haven't achieved anything yet.

I feel really helpless. Get a grip, I tell myself firmly. I can do this. And then I realize that I've got another problem to add to my list. Gran.

It's terrible walking along next to somebody, knowing that they only have about a year to live, and they don't know it. Maybe, if I could somehow get her to go to a doctor now, if it was picked up early enough, then she might not die. This realization is frightening. Could I somehow save Gran? As well as Sooty and my parents' marriage?

Suddenly everything is too much. What I would give right now to have my old problems back. Seth's betrayal, Mum's nagging, and the row with Imogen would all be bliss compared to what's facing me now. At the time, I thought my life was awful and that it couldn't get any worse. Now I feel embarrassed that I made such a fuss about such pointless things.

When we get home I follow Gran into the kitchen, because I can't bear to let her out of my sight. It's a bit like finding a precious jewel in a dung heap. I nearly trip over Gran's suitcase, which is standing in the hallway. I wish she didn't live so far away.

"I'll just have a nice cup of tea before I call the hospital," she says, putting the kettle on. "Would you like some juice?"

"I'd rather have a cup of tea," I tell her.

"Okay, one tea coming up."

I remember that the thing I liked most about Gran was that she always treated me like a grown-up. Which is a huge relief now, of course. Maybe I can really talk to her after all—even try and explain what's happening. But then she hands me my tea, which is way too weak with too much sugar in it. It's "baby tea," I realize, because her own cup is nice and strong. She might pretend to treat me like an adult, but she obviously still sees me as a little kid.

We sit opposite each other at the kitchen table. I can't stop staring at her. It is a bit like having tea with a ghost.

"Why so serious?" asks Gran.

"Well," I say, nibbling on a fingernail, "basically, my life is about to go down the pan. I think that Mum is going to throw Dad out and that we'll have to move to a horrid house and Mum won't be able to cope especially since—" I'm about to say "you've got cancer" but manage to stop myself just in time.

"Blimey!" says Gran with a twinkle in her eye. "That's a lot of weight to be carrying on such small shoulders." Then she sees my face and suddenly becomes serious. She reaches over the table and holds my hands.

"Listen, Alice, I know this new baby is going to mean that life will change a bit for you and that you'll have to share Mummy from now on, but don't look at it as a bad thing. It will be lovely to have a little sister to look after—"

"It's a boy," I interrupt.

"Or a little brother," she continues, "but I'm sure that everything will carry on just as normal."

Of course, I hadn't really expected Gran to take me seriously, and although it's a relief to say these things out loud, I'm still upset that she thinks it's all nonsense. She must have seen my disappointment because she squeezes my hands and says, "If there is one thing I'm certain of it's that your mum is *not* going to throw your dad out, so you don't need to worry on that score." She gets up and goes to the cupboard to find the cookie tin. When she's got her back to me I hear her mumbling, "More's the pity. She's a fool when it comes to that man."

"You don't like him?"

She turns around looking guilty and says, "I didn't say I didn't like him, but I won't pretend I was happy when your mum married him. He's not what you would call good marriage material." Suddenly she seems to realize that she's talking to a seven-year-old and laughs. "Anyway, I'm sure it will work out fine. It has so far."

"But what if it doesn't? Could you talk to them?"

"It's not my place to interfere," says Gran briskly. "Now, if you've finished your tea, I'll go and call the hospital."

"No, wait!" I grip her hands so she doesn't get up and disappear. She's the first person not to treat me like a child and I want to make the most of it.

"What is it?" she asks. "Not more problems, I hope," but she's smiling and I know she doesn't mind.

There's something that's been bothering me, even with everything else that's been going on. I decide to run it past Gran.

"Okay, say there was this boy at school and I really liked him and we started playing together and I thought he liked me, but then I heard this girl say that she'd bet him all her pocket money that he couldn't . . . couldn't . . ." obviously I can't say "get into her pants," so I finish, "erm . . . kiss me."

Gran looks thoughtful.

"Well, first of all I'd say the girl was probably jealous. Maybe she saw the boy playing with you and didn't like it and bet him her pocket money to kiss you because she wanted to spoil things. Did he try to kiss you?"

My mind goes back to the night in the park. Oops, I'm in

danger of losing focus here. Must concentrate. Yes, he kissed me, but that's not what we're really talking about here. He didn't try and get into my pants, which is what the bet was.

"No," I say, "we just had a nice time playing."

"Well, then," says Gran, "if I were you I'd ignore the girl and what you heard, and listen to your heart. If you think he likes you he probably does, so you should carry on playing with him. Don't stop on account of some silly girl."

Of course! I know in my gut that Seth did like me and wasn't pretending. And to think that I was going to let that stuff Sasha said ruin it for me. I can't believe I was stupid enough to believe her. I look gratefully at Gran.

"You're right," I tell her. "Thanks."

"No problem," says Gran. I see that she looks tired. God! How could I be so selfish! I've been going on about myself and my stupid problems, problems that don't even exist anymore, when it's Gran I should be thinking of.

"Gran?"

"Yes, love?"

"Listen. I had a bad dream last night. I dreamed you were ill and you wouldn't go to the doctor. It was really scary, Gran. Please, please, please will you go to a doctor and then I can stop worrying."

Gran laughs.

"Good heavens," she says, "I think we'd better get you a crystal ball." She drags the now cool teapot over and, placing it between us, puts my hands on it like it's a crystal ball. Then she laughs again. "Can you see anything else in the tea leaves, Gypsy Alice?"

"Gran! I'm serious!"

"That's what's so funny," she says. "The thing is, I have been feeling out of sorts lately and I went to the doctor, so don't worry."

"What did she say?"

"Well, she's not sure what's wrong with me so she's doing

tests. I'm sure it will be fine." She doesn't say this last bit with any conviction, though, and when I study her face, she doesn't look worried like you'd expect—she looks sad. And then I know that she knows about the cancer and all the planning in the world isn't going to change this one.

"Don't cry," she says, using a finger to wipe away the tear that's running down my cheek. But she doesn't try to make light of it, she just looks even more sad.

"Listen," she goes on, "if there's one thing I've learned in life it's that feeling sorry for yourself is a big waste of time. If there's something about your life that you don't like, then change it, and if it really can't be changed, you have to learn to live with it. Moping or getting angry just makes life unpleasant."

I can see her mentally shaking her sadness off and focusing her eyes back on me.

"Now that," she says, "is strictly between you and me. I don't want your mum worrying about me while she's got a new baby to look after." She stands up. "I'm going to call the hospital and see if that baby's made an appearance yet."

Sooty marches into the room and stands at the back door meowing. Gran goes across to let him out.

"Wait!" I shout. Her hand stops midway to the door handle. "Sooty isn't allowed out," I tell Gran.

I've just had an idea. If he doesn't go out at all, he can't get run over.

"What do you mean?" asks Gran.

"He mustn't go out. The vet said. Mum was going to get him a litter tray this morning. She must have forgotten."

"Oh my," says Gran. "What a palaver. He does look pretty desperate."

"Don't panic," I tell her, diving for the cupboard under the sink, where I pull out an old roasting pan that Dad ruined on the barbecue. "We can use this for now." I hand it to her. "I'll hold Sooty while you fill it with soil from the garden."

"Goodness, you are a resourceful girl," says Gran, obviously impressed. She's not the only one. I'm pretty impressed by my quick thinking as well.

I grab Sooty so that he can't escape out of the door when Gran goes out to get the soil. He doesn't like it and struggles to get free.

"Stop it," I tell him. "I'm doing this for your own good. It's not forever. Just until Mum gets back."

He scratches the back of my hand, but I don't mind. For the first time I feel like I'm actually doing something to change things.

I leave Gran to call the hospital and go up to my room. I need some time to think about what's happened.

I dig out the notebook and look at the list.

1. *Stop Sooty from getting run over.*
2. *Stop Mum and Dad from splitting up.*
3. *Find a way to get back to reality (¿)*
4. *Make Sasha's life hell.*

I'm tempted to check off number one, but decide I'd better wait. I don't want to tempt fate.

Number two is still a problem. I never did get to the library to get those marriage guidance leaflets, or the Gambler's Anonymous stuff. I haven't done enough. All I've done about it so far is to listen to Mum and Dad arguing. I suppose I did try and get Dad not to go out. Big deal. It didn't even work. Okay, so what have I learned from their arguments?

a) That Mum's unhappy about Dad going to the pub and the bookies so much.

b) That Dad's unhappy about Mum nagging him all the time and me whining.

That seems a bit unfair. After all, it's his behavior that's making us nag and whine. Or maybe it's the fact that we nag and whine that's driving him out of the house and to the pub and the bookies. God! I don't know.

It's all very well for Gran to say it's not her place to interfere, but this is my life we're talking about! I have to interfere.

I will make my parents stay together if it's the last thing I do. I just haven't worked out how yet.

I slump back on to the bed and consider number three. *Find a way to get back to reality (?).* Obviously if I'm going to achieve number two I can't work on this one yet. Besides, I'm not sure I know what "reality" is anymore. I don't think I believe in the coma theory. I mean, everything is too real. I'm not here in my mind—I'm definitely here in body. Maybe I'm in some sort of parallel universe. What if I can't get back? Will I always be mentally seven years ahead of myself? When I reach fourteen in this world will I actually be twenty-one?

Now I've worked out that Seth does like me, and all that stuff Sasha said was probably her just being horrid, I really want to get back and call him. Oh, my God! What if I have to wait seven years before I see him again? What if I manage to keep Mum and Dad together and then—in this world—Dad gets a new job and we have to move away? Then I'd never even meet Seth.

What if everything happens exactly as it did before and then, when I finally reach fourteen (again), and I'm in the park after Sasha's party and I fall off the merry-go-round again and end up back here again . . . Oh, God! I can't even think about that one!

What was it that Gran said earlier? "If you can't change something then you have to learn to accept it and make the most of it" or something like that. And not feel sorry for yourself. Right. Moving on, then.

I look at number four on the list.

4. *Make Sasha's life hell.*

I put a line through it. I'm not going to do that anymore. I don't like the way it makes me feel. I'm not a bully and I don't want to turn into one. And it's not because I'm really fourteen and feel like I'm picking on a little kid, it's because I don't want to turn into one of those girls that makes herself feel big by making other people look small.

I admit I'm feeling quite pleased with myself for this mature attitude when Gran calls up the stairs and says it's time to go to the hospital.

Chapter Seven

When Gran drops me off at school the next day she says, "Your mum and baby brother will be coming home today. Won't that be nice?"

I put on my best "happy" face. I've been doing a lot of that lately—pretending everything's just fine when really it's anything but.

As soon as I get into the playground, Sasha comes bounding up. "Well?" she says.

"Well what?" I reply. If she starts on about the skipping rope again I won't be held responsible for my actions.

"The baby! Has your mum had the baby? What is it? What's it called?"

So I have to go off into Baby Enthusiasm again, only now I'm quite enjoying it. I tell her it's a boy and that he's called Rory and that even though he's a bit scrunched and red he's actually quite sweet.

At the hospital last night, something occurred to me. Something major.

In the car, as we were driving to see the new baby, I was still congratulating myself on the fact that I'd decided not to be a bully. All the way there Gran was going on about the baby and how nice it was going to be for me. I had to pretend to be all excited because I didn't want her to think I was jealous or anything. It's only Rory, for God's sake! I was thinking. Anyone would have thought that Mum had just given birth to the second messiah, the way Gran was going on.

Dad was there when we arrived, but he soon made himself scarce.

"Have to go and wet the baby's head with the lads," he said as he backed out of the room. I had a sudden image of Trish ranting on the other end of the phone that Dad had disappeared. I wondered if he was about to do the same to us, which was silly really because I know he didn't.

I followed him out into the corridor and could just see him disappearing around the corner into the waiting area. I hurried after him, thinking that I was too late and that he'd have gone, but when I turned the corner I could see him standing outside talking on his phone.

I pushed the heavy doors open and walked up behind him.

"Okay, I'll see you in about half an hour. I'll stop off on the way and pick up a bottle of wine."

"See you later, Dad," I said, trying not to sound like I was whining. He spun around like I'd stabbed him with a red-hot poker.

"God, Alice—you nearly gave me a heart attack!" He didn't take the phone away from his ear. "I'm just arranging to meet the lads." He spoke into the phone again. "Right, I won't be long. Bye." He hung up the phone. "What are you doing following me out here? Run along back inside to your mum."

"You will be home before I'm asleep, won't you?"

"Sure I will, Princess," he said. Somehow I didn't believe him.

But he hadn't just disappeared all those years ago, I thought. That's not what happened. Still, I felt uneasy as I went back inside. Something was wrong, but I couldn't put my finger on it.

As I was walking through the waiting area, I spotted a huge rack of leaflets. I remembered that I hadn't been able to get to the library. Maybe there was something here that would be useful. It only took me a few minutes to find exactly what I needed. I ended up with two leaflets on alcohol abuse, one about the impact it had on your health and the other on getting help, including a flyer on support groups, that were held in the hospital. I didn't take the one on binge drinking as I didn't think it applied to my dad. I had one on gambling addiction, again with information on support groups, and I also found one on postnatal depression. As I made my way back to the ward, I was feeling very pleased with myself.

I stuck the leaflets into the back of the waistband of my skirt and pulled my sweater over them.

Mum was holding Rory and he was crying. Nothing changed there then, I was thinking. "Bloody baby" was my next automatic thought. Mum said to him, "Look, Rory. Here's your big sister."

And it was then, when I leaned over him, that I thought about the description he was going to write about me in seven years' time—the one I found in his homework book—and I felt ashamed. Some big sister I was going to turn out to be. He looked so small and defenseless and I wanted to protect him.

Then I realized that I wanted to protect him from *me*. That is, the me that I used to be. Or am going to be. Anyway, the me that he wrote about as being big and scary.

And that's when the major thing happened. I realized that there I was, thinking I was great because I wasn't a bully, when in fact I was! I'd spent the last seven years "bullying" this tiny baby. Okay, so he'd grown into an incredibly annoying child, but whose fault was that? Maybe if I'd been nicer to him he wouldn't have been so annoying.

All this thinking has got me through the bell and lining up and now we're in the cloakroom. I'm just taking off my coat when Clara and Chelsea grab me and drag me off to a corner.

"We thought you weren't speaking to Sasha," they whisper accusingly at me. I tell them what she did for me yesterday— about the ball and going to see Miss Strickland—and that she's a good friend. They look suitably impressed by this self-sacrifice, if a little disappointed that the hate campaign has come to an end. I'm tempted to tell them that in a few years' time they'll be Sasha's bosom buddies, hanging on her every word.

As we file into the classroom and I plonk myself down next to Sasha, I'm feeling a tad depressed. To be honest, the novelty is wearing off, and I'm getting a bit sick of hanging around with kids. I'm going to have to give some serious thought to the idea that this will not come to an end and that I'm really stuck here.

It's then that I have an idea, and I don't know why I didn't think of it before. What if I go back to the park and spin on the merry-go-round? I might fly off and find myself back where I should be. As soon as I've sorted Mum and Dad out I'm going to try it.

I'm just getting quite excited by this idea when Miss Carter comes in, followed by a strange girl. I'm not really concentrating until she says, "I'd like you all to welcome a new girl to the class. Say a big hello to Imogen, everyone."

Oh, thank God! I nearly shout out "Imogen, over here!" until I realize I'm supposed never to have seen her before. Still, I'm so excited I'm bobbing up and down in my seat.

"What's up with you?" says Sasha. "It's only a new girl. She looks really boring, if you ask me."

Before I can reply, Miss Carter says, "Alice, I'd like you to be Imogen's 'buddy' for a couple of weeks, until she gets settled in. Would you like to move over here and sit next to her?"

She's smiling at me in a conspiratorial way and I realize that this is what she was referring to when I went to see her about Sasha bullying me. She said she'd do something about it, and this is her way of moving me away from Sasha.

I've got such a big grin on my face it's beginning to ache. It's so good to see Imogen. As I get up to move, I catch sight of Sasha's expression. She looks close to tears.

"It's not fair," she's muttering. "You're *my* friend."

Not anymore, I'm thinking as I scoot across the classroom and sit down next to Imogen. Everything's going to be all right now, I think, smiling at her and trying to ignore the fact that she's only seven.

She looks very neat in her school uniform and her hair is cut in a shoulder-length bob with bangs.

She's looking at me through her bangs and I get the feeling that she's assessing me. It's very weird to think that this is the first time that Imogen has seen me. I want to make a good impression, but all I can think of to say is "hello" and to give her what I hope is a friendly smile.

"Hi," she says back. I wonder what I'm going to talk to her

about. She doesn't look like the kind of girl who would have a room full of Barbie dolls.

Playtime is a bit awkward. I'm trying to talk to Imogen but she isn't saying much. Maybe she's shy. It is her first day at a new school after all, and that must be scary. Sasha keeps butting in. I don't know why, but I sort of thought that she'd disappear and leave me and Imogen alone.

I can tell they've taken an instant dislike to each other. I'm tempted to tell Sasha to just go away but I don't, for two reasons. The first is that I don't think it would work. She's not going to give up that easily. The second is my vow not to be horrible to her, and this is really difficult to keep. I'm trying to remember why I came to this decision. Okay, so she stuck up for me and took the blame with Miss Strickland. Apart from that, I don't actually like her very much so the temptation to tell her to shove off is overwhelming. In an attempt to keep the peace, I suggest we all play a game of Puppies. Sasha is the owner, I'm the puppy, and Imogen has to be the shopkeeper and the vet.

The whole thing is a disaster. Imogen isn't very good at pretending and, for that matter, neither am I. I feel a real idiot panting, wagging my tail, and yelping. Sasha and Imogen are glaring at each other the whole time, and I think we're all relieved when the bell finally rings and we can go back inside.

Lunchtime isn't any better. Sasha is now being openly hostile toward Imogen and I know Imogen well enough to see that she's just biding her time, and it won't be long before she feels comfortable enough in this new school to start being horrid back.

Sasha suggests we play a game of hide-and-seek and tells Imogen to count while we go off and hide. Her motive becomes clear as soon as she's dragged me behind the caretaker's shed.

"Come on, let's run off and leave her," says Sasha, pulling on my cardigan.

"I can't, I'm her buddy, remember."

"So what," says Sasha, poking her head around the shed to see if Imogen is coming. "Quick, before she finds us."

"Look, Sasha," I say firmly, "I don't want to, okay. Anyhow, I *like* her."

Sasha looks completely gobsmacked. "You *like* her?"

"Yes."

"What, more than me?"

"Yes, more than you." I say this without really thinking, because it seems so obvious to me. But it's a huge shock to Sasha and she actually starts to cry. Oh, my God, I've made a little kid cry!

I try to put myself in her position. She's seven and her best friend has just told her that she doesn't like her anymore. She doesn't know anything about how she's going to be horrible to me all through secondary school so that it's hardly surprising that I don't like her. Also, I think I'm beginning to see why she's going to be horrible to me and I can't say I blame her. If my seven-year-old self just ran off with Imogen and left her on her own without a backward glance, it's no wonder she ends up hating me. All the same, that's hardly a good excuse for doing what she does. I mean, for God's sake, get over it!

She's about to run off and, I suspect, hide in the cloakroom and cry for the rest of playtime. I grab her hand.

"Look, Sasha, I'm sorry. I didn't mean it like that. What I meant was—I like her as well."

"I don't know why, she's horrible," Sasha says. I feel like screaming with frustration. And it doesn't end there.

When it's Sasha's turn to count, Imogen follows me as I hide behind a wall.

"I don't think Sasha likes me," says Imogen. "She's very bossy. I don't know why you put up with her."

I'm about to say "I don't either" when I stop myself. I can see how this is going to develop. Sasha and Imogen are going to fight over me until I choose one or the other. Obviously, the first time I was seven I chose Imogen. It would be so easy to do that again. But something is stopping me. I realize it isn't so much that each one is desperate to be my friend. It's not *me* they're fighting over. They just want to get one over on the other.

I look around the playground at all the other children playing happily together and I'm suddenly sick of both of them. I don't see why I have to pick one or the other. Why can't we all be friends? Not that that's going to happen. These two obviously loathe each other. What if I don't choose either? I think back to my fourteen-year-old self. I'm pretty certain that I don't want to be friends with Sasha because that would mean becoming one of the Handbag Brigade in secondary school, and I'm definitely not cut out for that. On the other hand do I really want to choose Imogen?

The thought of *not* choosing Imogen actually leaves me breathless for a few moments. What if I didn't? I know what will happen if we do become best friends. It will be me and her from now on. Exclusively. And while that used to make me feel important, now I'm not at all sure that's what I want.

I remember how I felt when Seth came to our school and I couldn't talk to her about it or even tell her that he'd asked me out. Also I start to remember some of the things she said to me during our argument. About how she was sick of me always being fed up with my life and taking it out on my mum. I wonder if I ought to tell her that if we become friends she'll get sick of me. Then there's the fact that I hardly ever saw her outside of school and that my social life was nonexistent. Not to mention the fact that she's about to go off to boarding school and abandon me! Is this really what I'd choose again? I'm not sure that it is.

"Why aren't you running?" Sasha appears around the corner. "You're supposed to run." She glares at Imogen, who's standing beside me. "You can't play anything right. I'm glad Miss Carter didn't make me your buddy. You're a hopeless loser."

Imogen just stares at Sasha with a cold-level stare, a bit like a panther watching its prey as it crashes through the undergrowth. I'm about to tell them both where to go, but something is stopping me. I realize that I want to resolve this with a bit of dignity.

* * *

Gran picks me up at three o'clock.

"Your mum's home with the baby. I'm just going to make sure she's settled in and then I'll have to go home."

"Oh no, can't you stay a bit longer?" I don't want Gran to go and leave me with Mum and Dad and the baby. Maybe they won't argue in front of Gran. Mum is hardly going to throw Dad out when Gran is there.

Gran puts her arm around me. "I have to get back to work. They don't give grandmas maternity leave. I'll come and see you next time I've got some holiday."

"But it will be too late by then," I want to shout at her. Instead I end up bursting into tears. And to make matters worse, I can't explain to Gran that I've just realized I might never see her again, so when she presses me to tell her what's upsetting me, I end up telling her about Imogen and Sasha instead.

"That all sounds a bit awkward," she says sympathetically. "Can't you be friends with both of them?" Honestly. Sometimes adults are so thick! I explain that this is not an option as they hate each other and always will.

"Always is a terribly long time," says Gran. "You never know, they might end up being the best of friends." Yeah, right, and I might end up being the next prime minister.

"Anyway," Gran continues, "don't feel you have to be friends with the new girl just because the teacher has put you together. Only you know if she'll make a good friend or not."

I think about this the rest of the way home. I can't believe that I'm actually considering not being friends with Imogen. It's a scary thought. I mean, she's my best friend. What would I do without her? Immediately quite a few things pop into my head. Have other friends, for starters. Go to the cinema with them. Have sleepovers. Talk about boys.

I realize that I've made up my mind what to do.

When I get indoors there's a party atmosphere in the air. Gran's made a cake to celebrate the new baby, and a couple of Mum's friends have come around for a cup of tea and to look at the baby. Mum looks tired but happy and I wonder when this postnatal depression is going to set in.

I go up to my bedroom and dig out the leaflets I picked up at the hospital last night. I take out the one on postnatal depression. I'm going to give it to Mum later, when her friends have gone.

The other ones are for Dad, but I don't have the nerve to give them to him. I go back downstairs and leave them lying on the coffee table in the living room where he'll see them, and then I go into the kitchen to have a piece of Gran's cake.

After dinner, which Gran cooks, I help her wash up and then I go to the shed in the garden and dig out a long piece of rope that Mum used to use as a clothes line before she bought the rotary one. I wind it up and force it into my schoolbag. I'm about to go into the living room where Mum and Gran are watching something on television, when the phone rings. I automatically pick it up. It's Dad. I look into the living room and see that Mum has Rory clamped firmly to one of her breasts.

"Mum's feeding Rory right now," I tell him. "Do you want to speak to Gran?"

"God, no," says Dad. "Just tell them that I've had too much to drink and I don't think I should drive home so I'm going to stay with a mate tonight. Okay?"

"Okay." I can't really think of anything to add. Usually, when Dad's had too much to drink, his voice gets really loud and jolly. I can't help thinking he sounds like his normal self. Maybe what he means is that he's *going* to have too much to drink.

"You're a good girl," he says, and hangs up.

I go into the living room and deliver the message. It gets a mixed reaction. Rory starts crying, but obviously that has nothing to do with the fact that his father is not coming home tonight. Mum moves him on to her other breast and he shuts up. Gran's lips disappear into a thin line—just like Mum's will when I'm fourteen and have done something she disapproves of and I know she's trying not to say what she really thinks. Mum looks embarrassed and I don't think it's got anything to do with the fact that one of her boobs is hanging out. As she tucks it away, she smiles weakly at Gran.

"Well!" she says with a forced cheerfulness. "That's a blessing in disguise. Alice can share my bed and you can have hers tonight. I'm sure you'd rather not sleep on the sofa again."

"Absolutely," says Gran enthusiastically. I know they're doing this for my benefit and I wonder what they'd be saying if I wasn't in the room. I wonder if Gran would stick by her resolution not to interfere or whether she'd voice her thoughts as to what a loser Dad is. Probably not. It wouldn't really help the situation.

"I wish I didn't have to go tomorrow," Gran says to Mum. "But I really have to get back to work. Are you sure you'll be all right?"

"We'll be fine," she says.

But nobody looks convinced.

Chapter Eight

At school the next day, Sasha pounces on me the minute I get through the gate.

"Why don't you tell Miss Carter that you don't like the new girl and ask her to make someone else her buddy?" she says to me.

I smile noncommittally. Imogen arrives and comes straight over. The two of them talk to me as if the other wasn't there. It's very tiring.

We spend the whole morning working on an art project, which is great because nobody notices how bad I am at art. I can paint away happily with the rest of them and my work looks quite good beside theirs. At break, Miss Carter asks for two volunteers to stay in and clean up.

Obviously no one is keen to give up their playtime to wash out a load of paint pots and brushes and only Henry Trotter puts his hand up. He's a puny lad who, I happen to know, is going to turn into an übergeek and he doesn't like playtime because he hates football and gets teased by the other boys.

I casually raise my hand. I could do with a break from the "terrible two." But when Sasha sees me, she quickly puts her hand up, too. Then, of course, Imogen does as well. Miss Carter looks surprised by the number of volunteers.

"Heavens!" she says. "You are a keen bunch."

She looks around the room. Please pick me and Henry, I'm praying. Sasha has her hand up so far she looks as though she's trying to touch the ceiling. Imogen has a determined look and is staring hard at Miss Carter. I don't want to get stuck with either of them.

But Miss Carter doesn't pick me at all. She picks Sasha and Imogen. Brilliant! I could laugh with glee at how that turned out. I couldn't have planned it better myself. But I try to look disappointed before I head out of the door into the cloakroom, where I grab the rope from my bag.

Out in the playground, I round up some of the girls. I start with Lucy and Miranda and persuade them to take one end of the rope each. As I start skipping, more and more girls want to join in, and by the end of the break there are about fifteen children playing skipping, including a few of the boys. It seems that I've started a new craze. I can see it being popular for quite a few weeks. The beauty of it is that, while we're all playing together, Sasha and Imogen won't be able to fight over me. They'll have to join in and I can be nice to both of them, while slowly easing my way into a different group of friends. They can either come with me or not, and if they don't, that will be their decision—so it won't look like I'm rejecting either of them. Perfect.

At home time, I'm in a really good mood. A lot of kids come up to me to check that I'm going to bring the skipping rope tomorrow. As I'm getting my things from the cloakroom, it occurs to me that that everyone is happy and excited and that, at the age of seven, that's a cool way to be. I think of everyone at fourteen, when it's not cool to get excited about anything and being happy doesn't seem to be cool either. Unless you're Luke O'Connor, that is. My fourteen-year-old self was hardly ever happy, though thinking about it now I don't know why.

My good mood lasts all the way home with Gran, even though I know she has to leave us after tea. When we get back, Mum is upstairs with the doctor. I think she's having her stitches checked. It's not really something I want to think about too much. I'm in the kitchen with Gran when I hear the doctor come downstairs.

"I'll go and see the doctor out," I tell Gran, and dash out into the hall.

I catch the doctor just as she's opening the front door. She smiles vaguely at me and I know that if I don't act fast she'll be gone. I can't think of any way to introduce the subject in a subtle way so I just blurt out, "I think my mum has got postnatal depression."

She looks down at me as she passes through the door. "And who have we here?" she says. "Dr. Watkins?" as if she's talking to a seven-year-old. Well, okay, she is, so how am I going to get her to take me seriously?

"I read a leaflet on it and she's showing all the symptoms," I tell her in my best grown-up voice—sort of woman to woman.

"Well, doctor—next time I have a patient and I don't know what's wrong with her, I'll give you a call." And then she actually pats me on the head! Luckily for her she's shut the door and gone by the time I come to my senses.

The condescending, patronizing old trout!

Mum's coming down the stairs. "Rory's asleep," she says, "so let's you, me, and Gran have a nice cup of tea together."

The next hour is great as we sit around the kitchen table and I try not to think about that fact that Gran will be leaving soon and that if I manage to "get back to reality" I will never see her again. We're eventually interrupted by the doorbell. "It's busy around here today," says Mum. "That'll be the midwife. I'll see her upstairs."

I follow them and hang around while the midwife chats to Mum about Rory and his feeding patterns and I help her to weigh and measure him. The midwife is really nice and doesn't treat me like some half-witted kid, so when it's time for her to go, I tell Mum that I'll show the midwife out and I follow her down the stairs. I'm desperately trying to think how to bring up the subject of postnatal depression when the midwife starts talking to me about Rory.

"Do you like having a little brother?" she asks me.

"Yes, it's great, but he does cry a lot." This gives me an idea, so when the midwife has finished telling me that babies tend to do that I pipe up, "But he doesn't cry as much as Mum."

This revelation causes her to pause at the front door.

"Oh yes?" she says, looking back up the stairs to where Mum is dressing Rory after his examination. I must tread carefully.

"I know she loves the baby very much," I tell her, "but she seems very unhappy at the same time."

The midwife sits herself down on the stairs so that she's on the same level as me. "Okay, well, that can happen sometimes. It's called the 'baby blues' because your mum's hormones have had a bit of a shock and she will feel up and down for a bit."

That may be so, but I desperately need this woman to take me seriously. I had been trying not to mention the phrase *postnatal depression* because I didn't want her to use that amused face that adults put on when faced by a precocious child.

"What if it's not just that, though?" I ask her. "What if she is . . . what if she has"—there's nothing else for it—"postnatal depression?" I finish on a whisper and wait for the amusement. But it doesn't come. Instead the midwife looks deadly serious.

"That can sometimes happen," she explains. "Actually more often than people think. So I tell you what I'm going to do. I'll be coming once a week for a while to check up on Mum and baby and I'll keep an eye on the situation." She takes a small card out of her pocket. It's got her name and job title on it and a telephone number. "If you're *really* worried about your mum at any point, you can call me on this number, okay?"

I could kiss her. She didn't laugh at me. I wonder briefly why she didn't pick it up the first time around, because I'm fairly certain that Mum didn't get any help last time I was seven. Then it occurs to me that Mum is the sort of person who always puts on a brave face, and she probably made an effort to appear cheerful and capable every time the midwife came around.

Still, I'm feeling more positive after she's gone and I go and help Gran make dinner. I feed Sooty and hope that his enforced imprisonment is saving him from being run over. I've been a bit sneaky about making sure he doesn't go out. When Mum got back from the hospital, I took one of Rory's tiny little socks and taped it around his foot. Then I told Mum he'd hurt it while she was away and that the vet had told Dad to keep him in for a few days. Luckily she hasn't discussed this with Dad yet, because he hasn't been here enough.

I go outside to empty the litter tray and refill it. My theory is that if none of the grown-ups have to think about it they won't even notice it's there. Sooty is mostly happy to sleep on my bed, although he does get under it if Rory's crying gets too loud. When he gets fed up with not being allowed out, I sneak bits of ham and cheese into my room. If this goes on much longer, he's going to end up really fat.

All in all I'm feeling fairly pleased with my progress. I think I will soon be able to cross off *save Sooty* from the list. So now all I've got to do is save Mum and Dad's marriage and then get back to being fourteen.

I wonder what it will be like at fourteen with Mum and Dad still together. Will we still be living in this house? If so, I hope they get around to decorating. And I bet I can persuade Dad to buy me my own computer.

Things will be better, I just know it.

My good mood is soon ruined after dinner when it's time for Gran to go home.

When she says good-bye and gives me a hug, I cling on tightly and don't want to let go.

"Hey! I'll be back soon," Gran says. Then Rory starts crying and Gran pries my arms away and goes to give Mum a kiss. Mum hustles Gran out of the house and into her car and turns away before Gran's driven off. I think she's being a bit rude until I see that she's crying as well. The three of us stand in the hall bawling (me), wailing (Rory), and weeping (Mum). I realize that if Dad comes home now and sees us like this he'll probably go out again. This thought makes me cry even harder. Then I remember what Gran said about feeling sorry for yourself and how it's a waste of time. Immediately my tears stop and I feel a surge of something. I think it's determination.

If Dad's not here to look after us then I'm going to have to do it.

I find Rory's pacifier in the changing bag by the front door and pop it into his mouth, then I lead Mum into the kitchen and make her sit down while I make her a cup of tea. All the time I'm doing this I am actually still feeling sorry for myself. I mean, I'm not a saint. As I pour the milk into the tea, I'm thinking about how unfair everything is. Then it hits me. Not all adults are adult! Dad is not an adult. He's like a kid who wants to go out and play with his mates and doesn't want to face up to his responsibilities. It makes me so mad that I'm beginning to think that if Mum doesn't throw him out, then I will. No, stop it! I'm sure I'm here for a reason, and it has to be to save the marriage. I'm sure I wasn't sent back just to save Sooty.

I sit at the table with Mum while she drinks her tea. She's stopped crying now and so has Rory. I need to know if my support is going to be enough. I need to know that she isn't resenting Dad for not being here. I decide to be direct.

"Mum?"

"Yes, love?"

"You wouldn't leave Dad, would you?"

Mum sighs. "Alice, we've had this conversation before. I told you. Your dad's not perfect, I'm well aware of that, but I love him, we're a family and I'm not about to throw that away."

I'm missing something here. What's about to happen to change Mum's mind? It would have to be something pretty dramatic for her to change from loving woman to vengeful harpy overnight.

Oh, my God! That's it! Overnight! It's Dad! That's why he didn't come home last night. He's having an affair! I knew there was something bothering me about that phone call he made at the hospital. If he was calling his friends, why would he tell them he'd pick up some wine on the way if he was going to the pub? Also, when he called up to say he wasn't coming home because he'd drunk too much—firstly he wasn't drunk, and secondly there wasn't any background noise, which means he wasn't in the pub like he was supposed to be.

I go all cold and then all hot. I think I'm going to be sick. I make a dash for the sink. I mustn't throw up. I pour myself a glass of water, but when I try to drink it my hands are shaking so much that the glass rattles against my teeth.

Dad's having an affair and Mum finds out and that's why she throws him out! I feel like I'm in too deep here.

But I must have been sent back to stop this, so how am I going to do it? I *have* to stop Mum from finding out. Either that or I have to persuade her that it's not the end of the world. The trouble is—it feels like the end of the world.

"There's a girl at school," I say tentatively, because I don't want to alarm her, "and her dad was having an affair so her mum threw him out and now she's really unhappy and cries all the time."

Mum looks a bit startled by this revelation. "Really? Who is it?"

"Oh, nobody you know." This isn't working. I'll have to be more direct. "Mum? If Dad was having an affair, would you throw him out?"

"Alice, your dad is not 'having an affair,' as you so quaintly put it. And even if he was, I wouldn't throw him out. I've just had a baby, and ending a marriage is not something you do lightly."

"But what if he was, though?" I know I'm beginning to annoy her, but I have to know.

Mum raises her eyebrows as if to say, "Oh no, not again," and sighs. "If he had been unfaithful I'd be very upset, but I'd sit tight and wait for it to blow over. Listen, there's something I haven't told you. When you were born, Dad disappeared for a bit. I didn't know where he was and I was worried sick. Then he came back. He was just scared. He soon got over it. I don't think he'll disappear again, but he might make himself scarce for a bit. Just until he's got used to the idea. So don't worry about it. It will be all right once everything settles down. Now look at the time—you should be in bed."

I don't point out that it's the weekend and there's no school tomorrow. Instead I kiss Mum and Rory and go up to my room.

I'm still feeling worried. It's all very well Mum saying those things, and I expect she believes them. She obviously has no idea how upset she is going to be, and how she won't be able to forgive Dad.

I really need to make sure she doesn't find out. I can't think of a single way to do this, because I don't know how she's going to find out.

Okay, let's be logical. She's not suspicious about him not coming home last night, and if he does it again she won't catch on because she'll assume that he's "making himself scarce." Maybe she finds some incriminating evidence, like a receipt in his trouser pocket for a huge bunch of flowers that she never got. Isn't that what usually happens in films and books? Right, so all I have to do is go through his pockets myself and remove anything that could give him away. What if she sees them together? If I make sure I'm with her when she goes out I can keep my eyes open and distract her if I see them. What if someone else sees them and calls up and tells Mum? I'll have to make sure that I screen all the calls myself. This seems like a plan to me. And if all else fails and she does find out, I'll beg her not to throw him out. I'll paint a very bleak picture of what our life will be like if we have to leave this house and she has to be a single mother.

Having decided that one of these is bound to work, I feel a lot calmer. I fall asleep under the weight of Sooty, who's purring so loudly on my chest it feels like I'm purring myself.

Chapter Nine

It's dark when I wake up. I'm lying on top of the bed, still fully dressed and Sooty has gone.

I can hear voices. Loud, angry voices. My heart sinks. They're arguing. I want nothing more than to block out the noise, turn over, and go back to sleep, but I know that I can't. Maybe they're just arguing about money or where Dad's been. I suppose I'd better find out.

I creep onto the landing and peer through the banisters. They're in the living room and I can hear Dad.

"It's that bloody interfering mother of yours, isn't it? I've a good mind to call her up and give her a piece of my mind."

I can see him standing by the coffee table. He's holding the leaflets I got from the hospital and waving them at Mum, who I can't see.

"I'm sure she thought she was being helpful," I hear Mum say.

"Helpful! She's just bloody stirring it! How many times do I have to tell you? I DO NOT HAVE A PROBLEM! So I like to go for a drink with the lads, and I might like to put the odd bet on a horse, but that does not make me an alcoholic with a gambling problem. I'm just a normal bloke doing normal blokey things, for God's sake!"

"Yes, I know, love, I know that. Just put them in the trash and forget about them." She's using the same voice that she uses on Rory when he's seven and having a tantrum. I hope it has the same calming effect on Dad as it usually has on Rory.

My hopes are in vain. Dad is obviously spoiling for a fight. He rips the leaflets up and throws them in her direction. They scatter all over the coffee table and onto the carpet around it. He's really angry, and it's all my fault.

I should go down and tell him that I put them there—not Gran—and that I'm sorry and I realize he hasn't got a problem. Now that I know it's not the drinking or the gambling that makes Mum throw him out, I can see that maybe he's not an alcoholic or a serious gambler. Although I'm not sure about the gambling, considering the wedding reception held next door to the bookies.

I'm thinking that that's the end of it and I might be able to go back to bed. But Dad hasn't finished.

"All I'm asking is that I go out now and again. That's not too much to ask, is it?"

"No," says Mum in her best pacifying voice, "that's fine. I don't mind if you go out now and again."

I can tell that Dad is getting frustrated. He wants an argument and Mum's not giving him one. At least he's stopped shouting. Perhaps that's the end of it. I stand up carefully so I don't make any of the floorboards creak, and I'm about to creep back into bed when I hear Dad saying, "The thing is, I think we got married too young."

This doesn't sound good. I creep down the stairs. Dad has his back to the door so he doesn't see me position myself beside the living-room door.

"I never had the chance to enjoy my youth. I was stuck with a family and a mortgage too soon."

What's he going on about? I do a quick calculation. They got married when Mum was twenty-five and Dad was twenty-seven and they had me the year after. It's not like they were teenage sweethearts, for heaven's sake! Sounds like he's making excuses.

Then I realize where this might be leading.

If he's about to say what I think he is, then I need to be on hand so I can dash in and stop him. Please don't tell her, please don't tell her—I'm thinking it so hard I wonder for a second if I've said it out loud.

"Susan, I've met someone else. I'm in love with someone else."

This is where I'm supposed to dash in and . . . and what? It doesn't matter, anyway, because I'm rooted to the spot like a statue. What I really want to do is collapse onto the floor and curl up into a tiny ball, but my legs won't bend. It seems like the only part of me that is still alive is my heart, and that's beating so hard I think it's going to burst. Even though I knew about the affair, hearing him say it is making it too real. I can't imagine what Mum's feeling.

"What do you mean?" says Mum.

"I mean," says Dad slowly, "that I am in love with another woman."

There's a massive silence and I'm steeling myself for Mum to go ballistic, but she doesn't.

"What other woman? Who is it?"

"It doesn't matter."

Of course it matters! I wonder who the hell it is.

"I'd still like to know," says Mum. Well, that makes two of us.

"She's called Trish. You don't know her."

Trish! It can't be! That's not right. He didn't fall in love with her until after he'd left. This is all wrong.

"Okay." Mum sounds shaky but in control. "I understand this is a difficult time for all of us—with the pregnancy and the baby and everything—but if you agree not to see her again then I'm prepared to forget it ever happened."

Suddenly I don't want Mum to be all forgiving. Dad has lied to me. All these years he's let me think that Mum threw him out, when the truth is he up and left us! I can feel tears running down my face. Now I want to throw him out and I'm willing Mum to do the same, but she's still strangely calm.

"It's all right, Gary. Let's just put it behind us."

"No, Susan, you don't understand. I don't want to put it behind me. I want to be with Trish. I'm leaving you."

"You can't leave us! Gary, I love you."

"I'm sorry. I'm going now. I'll come back at some point and get my things."

Before I know it he's out in the hall heading for the door. I'm just standing pressed against the wall with my mouth open. He sees me as he's pulling on his jacket.

"I'm just popping out. Look after your mum." And he's gone. He didn't even say good-bye.

I walk slowly into the living room. Mum's on the sofa. She's got Rory in her arms. She must have been feeding him, but he's fast asleep now, blissfully unaware that he is now fatherless.

I'm so angry I can't speak. What sort of person would do that? Apart from a selfish, conniving, evil bastard.

I go and sit next to Mum. I think she's probably in shock. She's trembling, and I wonder if I ought to get her some brandy or something. I get up and go to the cabinet, where there are a few bottles, but all I can find is some whisky. I put a large amount into a glass and take it to her.

"Thanks, love," she says on automatic pilot. I help her raise it to her lips and she takes a sip and makes a face then downs the lot.

"It's all right. He'll come back. I know he'll come back." I know that she really thinks he will, and I want to scream at her that he's gone and he won't be coming back, ever. I wish she'd put up more of a fight, but sitting next to her, feeling her tremble, I realize she has no fight left in her. In the morning I'll call Gran and I think I might call that nice midwife as well.

I take the throw off the back of the sofa and cover her up, then crawl in beside her. We stay snuggled up for a long time. Nobody says anything. There's nothing to say.

I drift off to sleep, but I'm having a nightmare. I'm doing my final high-school exam and I'm in the hall at school and I know that I've been given the wrong exam paper, but I can't do anything about it because we're not supposed to speak during the exam. It's supposed to be English, my best subject, but all the questions are in Spanish and I don't even take Spanish. Then suddenly I'm standing in the middle of a vast moor and we're on a school trip and we're supposed to be orienteering, but I've been given the wrong map. I know it's the wrong map because I can see the other children have got the right map, but they won't let me look at it.

"You have to use your own map," they tell me and walk off, leaving me alone on the vast moor.

I wake up covered in sweat with my heart beating fast. Mum and Rory have gone and I'm lying under the throw with my head on a cushion. I sit up in a panic. Maybe they've left me, too! I press my hand to my chest as if that will somehow stop my heart from beating so hard, then try and breathe steadily. Of course, Mum hasn't left. She's gone upstairs to bed and, not wanting to wake me, has tucked me up on the sofa.

My nightmare still feels very real. But instead of being stranded on the moor, I'm stranded in this previous life and I can't find a way out. Dad gave me the wrong map.

All those years he made out that it was Mum who had thrown him out when all the time it was a big fat lie. He just didn't want me to know what a bastard he was. And Mum never spoke about it, so I carried on thinking it was her fault and I took it out on her.

Now I've failed. Dad's gone and he isn't coming back. We'll have to move and Mum's ill. I feel cheated. What's the point of me being here if I can't stop it all from happening?

What if I had known the truth? What could I have done to stop it, short of actually killing Trish? I suppose I could have found her and told her what a bastard Dad is. Yes! That's it.

I creep out into the hall and put my shoes on. It's just getting light outside. I can be at the park in about half an hour if I hurry. I'm going to get back on the merry-go-round and see if I can go back to the beginning. Maybe, I think wildly, I can go further back and stop mum from having another baby. I could slip her the Pill or something. Now I'm being silly—I need to calm down. All I have to do is start again, and this time I'll find Trish and make sure she doesn't fall in love with Dad. I'll tell her about the horrible wedding and how Dad's going to leave her, too. Whatever, I'm going to do it all over again, only this time I'll get it right. One way or another, I'll stop Dad from leaving. Now I know the truth, I'll stand a better chance. I'll keep going back until I get it right. I'll do it ten times if I have to.

"It has to work, it has to work, it has to work," I chant as I run through the empty streets.

It's not until I get to the park and I'm actually sitting on the merry-go-round that I start to have doubts. Why does it have to work? I'm so angry with Dad that I'm not sure I want him to stay with us.

I think back to all the times, after the divorce, when we were supposed to see him for the weekend and he'd call up and cancel. He always said it because he had to work. But what if it wasn't? Now I know what he's really like, I suspect it was because he couldn't be bothered. We probably cramped his style. He'd rather have been down the pub with his mates or loved up with Trish.

Can I really face going back and having to go through all that again?

The problem is, even though I hate him and would be happy if I never saw him again, Mum still loves him and wants him back. What's going to happen when she realizes that he's not coming back? I have to try for her sake. And if it doesn't work and nothing happens when I push the merry-go-round, then I'll just have to make the best of it. I'll have to help Mum until she gets better, and at least I'll have some more time with Gran.

Here goes. I push the merry-go-round around as fast as my seven-year-old legs will allow. I just hope it's enough. I jump on and think about going back in time. I think about the first time it happened and how I woke up in the park in my seven-year-old body. I focus on that with all my might because I'm scared that I'll go back too far. I couldn't cope with returning to being two or three years old!

It's when the merry-go-round stops and the rest of the world is spinning at lightning speed around me that I panic. Wasn't I going the other way before? I'm sure I was spinning counterclockwise the first time. I think about jumping off—I don't care if I hurt myself. Then the world stops spinning and the merry-go-round jerks into motion and I'm thrown clear into the unknown.

PART 3

Chapter One

This time when I hit the ground, I'm fully conscious. Perhaps it hasn't worked, I think—panic rising in me. I lie still for a while, hardly even daring to think. Then I realize that the half-light isn't because it's dawn—it's dusk—and absolutely freezing. That's not right if I'm still seven.

I sit up and investigate. Oh no! Boobs! Nice and snug in my bra. I don't bother looking any further. I'm not about to start looking in my pants in the middle of the park.

I've gone forward instead of backward! I'm fourteen again!

I'll have to try again—only this time I'll push the merry-go-round the other way. Then again, perhaps this is the way it happens. I mean, you can't go back to being seven if you're already seven, so now I'm fourteen I should be able to get back to being seven if I try again. Still, I'll push it the other way just to be on the safe side. I don't want to fall off and find that I'm twenty-one!

It's easier to push now I'm bigger, and I get up a good speed before jumping back on. I wait for the merry-go-round to stop and the world to start spinning. It's not until the merry-go-round has slowed down to a complete standstill that I admit to myself that it hasn't worked. I can't believe it! Why isn't it working? It's got to work—I need to get back. I try again and this time I push so hard I can hardly keep up with the merry-go-round and nearly land flat on my face. But I jump on and screw my eyes shut, willing it to work. The merry-go-round slows down and squeaks to a standstill.

I try three more times before I finally admit defeat.

I get off and try to think myself back to where I was before all this happened. If I remember rightly, I was in a desperate situation.

I couldn't go home where I'd fought with Imogen and Mum, and I couldn't go to Dad's because he wasn't there. I had nowhere to go and was considering staying the night in the park. Great. Here I am again. It obviously wasn't willpower that made me go back in time, and it can't have been sheer desperation or it would have worked again just now.

I consider my options. If I'm stuck here and fourteen again, what am I going to do? I remember how awful it was sitting here in the park and the row and Trisha being scary and Dad not being there for me. The old Alice felt like it was the end of the world and would never have considered going home and apologizing to Mum. This time, though, it doesn't seem like quite such a catastrophe. I don't have a problem with apologizing to Mum, especially if it means I can have a nice hot bath and go to bed. I'm seriously freezing out here. Also, I'm looking forward to seeing her again. It's seven years since I last saw her, if you see what I mean. I feel guilty that I messed up and didn't get to fix her and Dad after all. I feel cheated. I mean, what was the point in all that? Why go through the bother of being seven again if nothing's changed?

If I'm totally honest with myself, I'm quite relieved that I'm not seven anymore. I've escaped the aftermath of Dad walking out on us. I know I should be worried about getting back and fixing Mum and Dad's marriage, but deep down I'm glad that I don't have to face it again. I did my best, and even though I failed it's hardly my fault. I mean, I would have stood a better chance if I hadn't been lied to (by Dad) in the first place. All that crap about Mum throwing him out! He doesn't deserve us.

I feel a bit disoriented. Here I am, back in my old life, but I'm not the same person anymore. In fact—I'm a bit ashamed of the old Alice. She was such a brat. She behaved more like a seven-year-old sometimes than a fourteen-year-old. I think of all those fights she had with Mum. She wasn't a very nice person. In fact, I wonder if by being seven again, I've actually grown up a bit. How perverse is that?

I pick myself up off the ground and brush myself down.

It's then that I get a funny feeling that everything is not quite as it should be. Although it seems like a lifetime ago, I know exactly what I was wearing when this whole thing started. I had some black jeans that I got at the thrift shop with Imogen and a tie-dyed Joe Bloggs top. Also, I wasn't wearing a jacket, whereas now I am.

I won't deny that I feel a bit scared. Not because I'm on my own in the park—in the dark—but because I don't know what's going to happen next.

The rails on the merry-go-round gleam in the moonlight. I think about trying it one more time, but deep down I know it's not going to work. I'm stuck here, so I'd better get on with it. The first thing to do is get back home.

As I make my way through the bent railings and back toward George Street, my mind is still on what just happened. I think of Mum wrapped up on the sofa cuddling Rory, abandoned by Dad. I'm so furious with him. Should I have explained to Mum that he wasn't coming back?

It's no good thinking about that, because it all happened seven years ago, not an hour ago. I need to think about what's happening *now*. I turn into George Street and slow down to give myself time to adjust.

Last time I was here I had fought with Mum and Imogen and then run off. I'm halfway down the street and I can see that there are no police cars outside our house, so I assume there isn't a full-scale search going on for me. What am I going to find at home? Will Imogen still be there? Will Mum still be mad at me?

When I get to number twelve I nearly walk right past it. I stop and check the number on the gate. It's definitely the right house, but it's not like it was when I left. The hedge has been cut right down and there's a new gate. The front garden has things planted in it, which I assume are flowers, although as it's February they're not in bloom. Looking more closely, I can see that the window frames are no longer rotting. In fact, all the windows have been replaced with new ones. The whole house looks more inviting and it's only when I'm halfway up the path that I suddenly realize that it's probably because we don't live here! Oh, my God! That would explain the different clothes. I haven't come back to the life that I left. I've come back to a different one, and I don't even know where I live!

Chapter Two

I go hot and then cold. I creep up to the front door and peer through the mail slot. The hall light is on and I can see that the floor has been sanded and varnished and there are nice rugs down the hallway. The walls are no longer green; they've been painted a nice creamy color. I'm wondering what to do when the living-room door opens and a woman comes out into the hall. I look desperately to see if it's Mum, but it most certainly isn't, not unless she's put on about 80 pounds.

Before I can stand up and get myself down the path and away, she's steamed down the hallway and opened the front door. She lets out a little scream when she sees me kneeling on the doormat and puts her hand over her heart. God! I hope she isn't going to have a heart attack. Then I realize that I know her. It's Mrs. Archer from down the road. What's she doing here?

"Is everything all right?" There's another woman coming out of the living room. It's Mum! I could cry with relief!

"Alice, what are you doing home?"

They're both looking at me. I bend down and pretend to pick something up.

"I . . . um . . . dropped my key. I'm sorry if I startled you, Mrs. Archer." I move out of the way so that she can go.

"Bye, thanks again," says Mum as Mrs. Archer lets herself out of the gate.

I walk into the house and follow Mum down the hallway.

"Mrs. Archer came around to keep an eye on Rory. I had to go to the nursing home in a hurry." Some things haven't changed, then, I think as I follow Mum into the living room.

It's much nicer in here, too. All the heavy furniture has gone and the horrid, dark wallpaper. I'm just taking it all in when Mum comes up and gives me a hug. For a moment I think I'm seven again and glance down at myself to check. No. I'm fourteen and I hug Mum back tightly. I'm so glad to see her. I do wonder what happened to Imogen, though. She obviously isn't here.

"I'm sorry, darling," Mum is saying, "I had to go to the nursing home because Miss Maybrooke took a turn for the worse and she was asking for me. I only just got there in time. I'm afraid she passed away."

"Okay," I say hesitantly. I'm not sure what's expected of me.

"I'm sorry you weren't here, I expect you'd have liked to have seen her. I bet you're glad you visited her yesterday. I know she was like a grandmother to you, but at least she's not in pain anymore."

I sit down on the sofa to take all this in. Why would I have visited Miss Maybrooke? The old me would have had to be carried into the nursing home, kicking and screaming, before she would have visited an old lady. This me is clearly a nicer person.

I try and look suitably sad. And, to be honest, I *am* sad. I'm sad that the old me didn't make friends with Miss Maybrooke and go and visit her, that the old me was too busy being angry with Mum and self-obsessed and selfish to actually go out and get a life.

"I'll go and make us some hot chocolate," says Mum.

I'm relieved to be alone for a bit. My head is spinning. Where am I? Am I in a parallel universe? This is clearly my life, but it's not the one I left behind. There's a clock on the mantelpiece and it says eight-thirty. Time. It always seemed so constant and yet I've just traveled through it—twice. And now I don't know where I am.

I go out into the hall to hang up my jacket and I catch sight of myself in the hall mirror. Oh, my God! It's not even me! I've come back as a different person! When I've calmed down a bit and really looked at myself, I realize that it is me. Of course it's me. Mum's been calling me Alice, and she is my mum, so I am still me. I just didn't recognize myself in the mirror because my hair is dead short! I run my hand through it. There are some longer bits framing my face, but the top is sticking up like I've put gel in it and I swear it's been dyed because it's really blonde. I look "elfin" and, at the moment, a bit like a startled rabbit caught in the headlights.

The more I look at it, the more I like it. It suits me. I definitely look more sophisticated and older than the old me. It's weird, though. The old me would never have dared have a hairstyle like this. It makes me wonder exactly what this new Alice is like. I mean, I like this style, but am I going to be able to carry it off? I certainly feel more confident than I used to, but am I as confident as this? It's all very confusing.

I check out the hair one more time and use a bit of mascara from the wand that's lying on the shelf below the mirror. I look great and resolve to live up to this "new" image if it kills me.

Mum comes out of the kitchen carrying two mugs and I follow her back into the living room.

"So, what happened?" she says. "Was the party no good?"

I nearly choke on my hot chocolate. What party? The only party I know about is Sasha's, and why would I be going to that? Unless . . . Oh, my God! Don't say I'm part of the Handbag Brigade in this life!

Mum's looking at me expectantly.

"I . . . um . . . changed my mind. Decided not to bother."

That's when I see something glowing in the corner of the room. It's a computer. In our living room! I go over to check it out.

"Oh, I was just finishing off some work when I was called to the nursing home. I'll switch it off if you don't need it," says Mum.

I hit one of the keys and the screensaver disappears. There's a load of words on the screen, but the ones that jump out at me are *Key Stage 2*. Are they introducing SATs into the nursing home? Then I spot a pile of exercise books beside the computer. The penny drops.

"You're a teacher!" I say out loud before I can stop myself.

Mum gives me a funny look. "Well, duh, it was your idea," she says in an exaggerated teenage voice, which makes me laugh. "Where have you been for the last seven years?"

This makes me laugh even more. I stop suddenly when I realize that there's a slightly hysterical note in the laughter. I consider telling Mum where I've been, but decide against it. She'll only think I've gone mad. As it is, she's staring at me through narrowed eyes.

"Were there drugs at the party?" she says. She's trying to sound casual, but I can detect a hint of fear in her voice. I go over and give her a hug.

"I didn't go to the party, Mum, and I haven't taken any drugs."

"Sorry, darling. It's just that you have been acting strange ever since you got in."

I smile at her in what I hope is a reassuring way. I really have to get a grip. Act normal. Pretend everything is fine. In a way, this is harder than going back to being seven. I need to find out some stuff, like who I am now, and why Imogen isn't here, and why the house looks different, and how Mum got to be a teacher, and whose party was I meant to be at, and . . . the list seems endless and I feel like my head's about to explode.

It feels weird sitting here drinking hot chocolate with Mum. The old me would never have done this—we'd have been arguing within minutes. I try and remember what it was exactly that we argued about. It makes me tired just thinking about it. I must have wasted so much energy on hating Mum. It's so much better sitting here with her having a normal conversation. Except it isn't normal, because I don't know what to say. I lean back into the cushions and try to relax and enjoy the moment. The trouble is, I've got all these questions and I need to ask them without her thinking I'm mad.

I look around the room. "Do you remember all that old, dark furniture that was here when we moved in?"

"Oh, heavens, yes," says Mum. "Wasn't it gloomy?"

"What happened to it?"

"Well, if I remember rightly, you were a bit scared of it, so I plucked up the courage to tell Miss Maybrooke that it didn't really suit us and it all went down to the auction house."

The mention of Miss Maybrooke has just made me remember something.

"Oh no! Miss Maybrooke! The house! Are we going to have to move?"

"What are you talking about? Why would we want to move?"

"I just thought that maybe . . . with the house being hers and everything . . ."

Mum's giving me that look again. "Alice, I bought the house off her years ago. You remember? She gave us such a good deal. . . ."

"Oh yes . . . of course . . . I remember now. Silly me." I decide to change the subject quickly before she starts worrying about drugs again.

"Mum?" I'm wondering how to put this. "Can I talk to you about Dad?"

"I hope you're not regretting that you didn't go to his wedding, because it's a bit late now."

Ah, so in this life I refused to go to the wedding from hell. Thank God, I think, remembering the hideous ordeal of the pink dress and the sleazy pub.

"No, no, I'm not regretting that."

"So, what do you want to discuss, then?"

Good question. I don't really know. Luckily I don't have to worry, because Mum fills me in, anyway.

"Look, Alice, I'll be totally honest with you. The main reason I've insisted that you see your dad is really for Rory's sake. I know, if you'd had your own way, you wouldn't have had anything to do with him, but he is still your dad and I felt that Rory needed a male role model."

A picture of Dad in the pub showing Rory how to use the one-armed bandit springs to mind.

"I'm not sure he's the world's best role model," I tell Mum.

"Well, no—you're probably right, but he is Rory's dad, and that will never change. Still, I recognize that as you're nearly fifteen you do have a right to make up your own mind and I won't insist that you stay there anymore if you'd rather not. But don't write him off completely, because you might regret it one day. Just keep in touch, okay?"

"I don't understand how you can forgive him for what he did to us," I say. Dad walking out the door is still very fresh in my mind.

"Who says I've forgiven him?" says Mum. "The point is it was a long time ago and life goes on."

"Well, now Trish is pregnant he can make the same mistakes all over again," I tell her bitterly. I look over at her, expecting a reprimand for being rude about Dad, but instead she's gone all pale and drawn looking.

"What do you mean, Trish is pregnant? Are you sure? Who told you?"

Uh-oh, I've gone and put my foot in it. And I'm not even sure that Trish is pregnant in this life.

"I don't know for certain. I just sort of heard—maybe that's why they got married in such a hurry," I say, clutching at straws.

"Well, I hope you're wrong, for her sake," says Mum. Suddenly I'm bored with talking about Dad. I can't see that any of it has anything to do with us anymore.

Then the phone rings.

Chapter Three

Mum answers it and says, "Yes, she's right here," and passes it to me.

"Who is it?" I say frantically into the phone.

"Lucy. Why isn't your cell phone on?"

Lucy Clark? Why is she calling me? I thought it might be Imogen. I can only just hear the voice at the other end. There's a lot of noise in the background.

"Sorry, the battery's flat," I lie automatically. I don't even know where it is.

"Are you coming? We waited for you, but when you didn't turn up we went on to the party."

This calls for some seriously quick thinking. I need some information.

"The party . . ." I say vaguely.

"Sasha's party, remember? Don't tell me you forgot. It's all she's been talking about for weeks." Well, that sounds familiar, at least. "You have to come," Lucy continues. "It's just warming up."

"Right. Um . . . have I been invited?"

"What is wrong with you?"

"Am I friends with Sasha?" It comes out before I can stop it.

"Are you going senile or something?"

Great. Now she thinks I'm mad. Still, that could work to my advantage at the moment.

"Just humor me for a minute, will you?" I ask her.

"I know it's not like you're bosom buddies or anything, but let's face it—a party's a party. And it's not a bad one either, so get your arse down here, will you?"

I'm just taking in the fact that I'm not one of the Handbag Brigade after all. Thank God for that!

I can hear someone in the background saying, "Give me the phone," and then another voice comes on. "Where have you been? Where are you?" I think it's Miranda Wilkes.

"I'm in an alternative universe," I tell her.

"Yeah, right, whatever—you have to get here right now. It's a blast." Obviously, she's used to me sounding a bit crazy. I don't know whether to be relieved or worried by that.

I desperately try to think of an excuse not to go. I mean, these are obviously my friends, but I feel like I need time to get used to that idea before I go off to a party with them. I wonder if it's the same party I ended up at last time I was fourteen and if it's going to get invaded by party crashers.

Then it occurs to me; if it's Sasha's party then Seth will be there! My heart instantly overrides my head. Besides, I tell myself, what better way to get used to your new life than to throw yourself in at the deep end?

"Mum, can I go along to the party?"

She immediately comes over all Mumsy. "How are you going to get there? You can't walk there on your own at this time of night, and I can't take you because I can't leave Rory."

"I'll be fine, it's not far. I could cut through the park."

Wrong thing to say. "No, I'm sorry, Alice, but you can't go now, on your own. Why didn't you meet up with your friends like you were supposed to?"

"Look, it's no big deal! I can be there in ten minutes if I run," I plead. I really need to go—not only to see Seth but to find out what else is going on in this life of mine.

"No, Alice," Mum says with a finality that I recognize.

I put the phone back to my ear.

"Miranda?"

"No, it's Lucy again. Are you coming?"

"I can't. The Gestapo won't let me out on my own. It seems I have to be escorted everywhere like a *seven-year-old*," I say practically shouting the last bit.

"Oh, bad luck," says Lucy, "mine's exactly the same." A load of noise erupts in the background. "Got to go," she yells, and hangs up.

Tears of frustration are building up. I glare at Mum.

"I can't believe how unfair you are! Why can't you get Mrs. Archer back and then you can take me."

"Don't be ridiculous, Alice," says Mum. "The poor woman has only just gone home."

"I don't care. You are so mean," I tell her stomping to the door. "I hate you!" I yell and run up the stairs.

I can hear Mum saying "Alice?" in an exasperated voice.

I slam my bedroom door behind me. Whoa, what was that about? I'm behaving like a seven-year-old. Except I wasn't even that brattish at seven. Obviously, old habits die hard. Deep down I know I was being unreasonable and I shouldn't be taking it out on Mum. But I am disappointed about the party.

I want to see Seth again.

I'm staring at my bedroom. I can't believe how great it looks. I've still got the big mahogany bed, but it looks classy now that the walls have been painted a creamy white and the rest of the furniture is modern. It's not obsessively tidy, but it's nothing like the dump that my other room was. I definitely feel at home in here. It doesn't feel like a guest bedroom any more, that's for sure.

I wander around a bit uncertainly, like I'm snooping through someone else's property. I tell myself not to be silly. All these things are mine. I spot an MP3 player on the bedside table and when I flick through the index, it's got all my favorite songs on it, plus a few that I'm not familiar with.

Above the desk is a big bulletin board covered in photos. I spend a long time studying them. Most of them are of my friends. My "new" friends. There's one taken in this room of five girls having a sleepover. I reckon we're about ten or eleven years old. I recognize Lucy and Miranda and there's also Anna and Jade. Right in the middle is me, laughing madly at something. I really wish I'd been there.

There's no sign of either Sasha or Imogen. I look at all the other photos up there, school trips, birthdays, parties—no Imogen. It suddenly hits me. The decision I made the other day, when I was seven—not to be friends with her after all—this is the result! She's gone from my life—this life. She hasn't been a part of it. I feel quite weak at the thought and grasp the back of the chair. Then I spot her in the background of one of the photos taken on a school trip. She's standing apart from us (we're all making funny faces at the camera) and it's a bit difficult to make out because she's so small in the distance, but it's definitely her. She's not alone, though. There's another girl with her, but she's got her back to the camera and there's no way I can tell who it is. I feel a slight jab of jealousy. Or is it regret? Whatever it is, it's going to take a bit of getting used to.

I study a picture of Mum and Rory, which was taken on a day out somewhere. Mum looks relaxed and happy and Rory looks like Rory. I suddenly realize I've missed him.

I slip across the landing into his room. He has a nightlight that glows in the corner because he's afraid of the dark. He's fast asleep. I'd like to say he looks beautiful and sweet lying there, but actually he's all sweaty and he's drooling onto the pillow. I still love him, though.

Rory's bedroom looks exactly the same as it used to. I remember, in my old life, Mum offered to make my room better, but I think I went nuts and said, "What's the point?" I think she said something about cutting off my nose to spite my face, whatever that means.

I'm about to go back to my room when I spot Rory's schoolbag propped against a toy box. I rifle around inside and find his literacy book. I'm not really expecting to find what I'm looking for, but halfway through is a page headed *My Big Sister*.

My big sister is nice. Sometimes she looks after me and we have fun.

She takes me to the park and pushes me really high on the swings, but she won't let me go on the merry-go-round, she doesn't like it. I like it best when she reads me a story. She helps me with my reading and she smells nice.

I put the book back in the bag. There's a lump in my throat. I think about the promise I made to Rory in the hospital just after he was born because I was ashamed to be the person he wrote about the first time. It looks like this Alice kept the promise.

Chapter Four

Lying on my bed, I'm still glowing from what Rory wrote about me and staring at the pictures on the wall of all my friends, when I hear the door creak open. I turn and smile, thinking that Mum has popped in to say good night. I'd better apologize to her for taking it out on her. But there's no one there. I'm just scaring myself with thoughts of Miss Maybrooke's ghost when I hear a little meow.

"Sooty?"

He responds to the name and jumps up onto the bed and starts to rub his face on my arm. I can't believe it. Is this really Sooty? He's much bigger and heavier. He looks like an eight-year-old cat so I suppose it must be him.

I lie in the dark feeling Sooty's purrs vibrating through me and I'm aware of another feeling in my chest. It's so alien to the fourteen-year-old me that it takes me awhile to work out what it is. It's happiness. I feel happy.

Maybe I'm not in a parallel universe. Maybe, when I fell off the merry-go-round I died and this is heaven. No, it can't be, or I'd have a television in my bedroom. And my own computer. And bigger boobs. And a gorgeous boyfriend.

And then it hits me. This isn't a parallel universe at all. This is my life as it was, only now it's better because of the things I did when I went back to being seven. I saved Sooty and I helped Mum by getting her help for her postnatal depression.

The fact that I didn't abandon Sasha to be friends with Imogen means that now I've got a whole heap of other friends and Sasha doesn't hate me, or I wouldn't have been going to her party.

Did she really make my life hell because she never forgave me for what happened when we were seven?

But it's not only these things that have made a difference. The biggest difference is me. How come I wasn't happy before? I could have been if I hadn't been so busy feeling sorry for myself and hating Mum, when the divorce wasn't even her fault in the first place.

God! I wish someone had told me what a brat I was being. The sad thing is, even if they had I wouldn't have taken any notice. I was too busy feeling sorry for myself.

And now, here I am in the life I could have had before, if I'd just been a better person. I feel cheated because I never got to live that life—by getting on the merry-go-round and fast forwarding here, I sort of missed it. Instead, I had a horrid time from seven to fourteen and it could have been so much better if I hadn't ruined it by being such a brat.

I know I should be grateful that I'm here now, but it seems a bit unfair that I've missed all the fun. I resolve to make up for it by making sure that I have fun from now on. Not much hope of that, though, if I'm not allowed out!

Mum pops her head around the door. "There's someone downstairs to see you," she says.

I jump off the bed, startling Sooty, who curls back up in the warm spot.

"Who is it?"

"It's a handsome prince come to escort Cinderella to the ball," she whispers, grinning at me.

Oh, my God! Seth!

I do a quick check in the mirror and slap a bit more lip gloss on.

"I'm sorry I shouted at you," I tell Mum, and then dash out onto the landing. I stop myself from rushing down the stairs and try to descend gracefully. There's a boy standing in the hallway smiling up at me—but it isn't Seth. It's Luke.

I try not to look too disappointed.

"Hi there," he says. "I've come to take you to the party."

I turn to check with Mum that it's still okay to go.

"Sure," she says, "as long as you come back with someone. And be back at midnight. I don't want you turning into a pumpkin in public."

I kiss her and leave.

Chapter Five

It's a bit awkward walking down the road with Luke. I don't know what to say to him. I don't think it's my imagination, but he seems a bit tense as well.

"Thanks for coming to get me," I say.

"That's okay. It wouldn't have been so much fun without you." Is he blushing? My heart starts pounding. What if he's my boyfriend? It's hardly the sort of thing I can ask him. By now we're at the park and we have to walk around it to get to Sasha's. I don't know if I can put up with the uncertainty for that long.

"Shall we cut through the park?" I ask Luke. "There's a hole in the railings and it's a really quick shortcut."

Once we're in the park and the streetlights have faded, Luke becomes more like his old self. He runs off down the path and hides behind a tree, and when I get there, he jumps out on me and says in a creepy voice, "Hello, little girl, and where are you going all alone?"

I can't help laughing. When we get to the playground he jumps onto the merry-go-round.

"Come on, I'll push you," he says.

"No way, I'm not going on that thing," I tell him, backing off. He jumps off and, grabbing me by the hand, drags me over to it. Oh, what the hell, I think, getting on. It's only a stupid merry-go-round.

He jumps up next to me and I sit there grinning inanely at him, waiting for it to slow down. My heart is beating way too fast and I'm expecting the world to start spinning at any moment. I realize that I must look really scared and nervous when all we're doing is sitting on a merry-go-round. But it's no good, I'm not risking another time-traveling episode, and I jump off really quickly before anything disastrous can happen. Turning to Luke, I laugh nervously. No doubt he thinks I've gone completely mad.

It's then that I realize that in the split second before I jumped off, I swear he was about to kiss me! Now, he's sitting dejected on the merry-go-round, no doubt thinking that I jumped off to avoid being kissed! And I can't explain the real reason to him.

"We'd better get to the party," he says, jumping off the merry-go-round. "They'll wonder where we've got to."

But, as we make our way toward the railings, he takes my hand. Oh, my God! He *is* my boyfriend! What am I going to do? I try not to pull away. I like Luke and I don't want to hurt his feelings. I'll just have to sort all this out later.

I wonder how long we've been going out together.

When we get to Sasha's house, I'm half expecting to be greeted by the scary scenes that Seth and I encountered. But there aren't any crashers puking up on the lawn this time.

When we get inside, Lucy comes bounding down the hallway.

"Come on, you're missing all the fun." She grabs me and drags me into the living room. "You have to join in this dance with us," she shouts above the noise. A line of her mates are all doing a funny dance together and she plonks me on the end. I have no choice but to join in. I'd look a right fool just standing there otherwise.

Once I get the hang of the moves, though, it's a really good laugh. Luke is next to me on the other side and he's really going over the top, flinging himself around wildly. By the time the track has finished, we're doubled over laughing. Then another track starts and everyone is dancing together. The old me never danced, well, not in public anyhow. What the hell, I think, this is really good fun. No one cares if they look like an idiot. They're just having a good time.

Three tracks later we're all out of breath and flop onto the sofa. This is all very weird, but it feels right at the same time. I'm obviously a part of this group and I decide to just go with the flow. Miranda is sitting on one side of me and Lucy is on the other.

"I like your top," says Miranda, "Did you buy it this morning?"

I'm just about to say, "What? This old thing?" when Lucy pipes up, "Yes, I made her buy it. She was worried it was too lowcut."

Luke is hanging over the back of the sofa. "There's no such thing as 'too low cut,'" he says. Miranda hits him over the head and he disappears. We can hear mock groaning coming from the floor. I gaze down at my cleavage. And yes, I actually have some. Have I landed in this alternative universe with bigger boobs? On closer inspection I realize that they're the same size as my old ones.

"That bra is really good, too," says Lucy. "Aren't you glad I made you buy that as well?"

"I wish I could have come shopping, too," says Miranda, "but I couldn't get out of going to visit Grandad."

"Yeah, it was fun, wasn't it?" says Lucy, turning to me.

"The best," I tell her, really wishing I'd been there. Then I see Seth going past the door and my heart goes flip-flop. I decide to go and get a drink.

As I'm making my way toward the kitchen, I pass the study where Sasha was hiding at the first party. I can hear voices coming from in there. One of them is Seth's. Now I know it's rude to listen at doors, but let's face it, these are exceptional circumstances.

The other voice is Sasha's, and they're arguing.

"Our parents said no alcohol and they left me in charge, so if you go out and buy some, then I'm sending everyone home." That's Seth.

"God, you're so boring. Anyhow, it was your dad that said no alcohol, not my mum." Sasha sounds mega sulky.

"It doesn't matter who said it. The point is you're not allowed any, and if you get some they won't let you, or me, ever have a party again. You don't need to get drunk to have a good time, you know. There's loads of people in there having a great time, dancing and stuff. Why don't you go and join them?"

"What, you mean that lame lot, Alice and Lucy and their loser friends?"

"If they're so lame why did you invite them? They look fine to me."

"I suppose you fancy one of them, do you? I suppose it's Alice. All the boys fancy Alice."

They do? Wow.

"But I bet you fifty quid you can't get into *her* pants."

"God, you're disgusting sometimes. Why don't you just grow up?"

"Yeah, and why don't you just chill out? You sound like your dad."

"So? What's wrong with my dad?"

I decide I've heard enough and head into the kitchen. I'm just helping myself to some nonalcoholic punch when Seth walks in. I smile at him. He looks more gorgeous than I remember. My mind goes back to before, when we were in the park and he kissed me. I wonder what he'd do if I walked over to him now and kissed him. I can feel my smile getting bigger as I contemplate this idea. Then I realize that I must look like a complete idiot, clutching my glass and grinning at him like a maniac.

I needn't worry, though. He's looking at me but not seeing me, if you know what I mean. He smiles politely but his mind is elsewhere.

I want to wave my arms around and shout, "Hello! Over here! I'm your girlfriend, remember?" But he doesn't remember because that happened in the other life. We only went out twice—once for coffee and once in the park. Does that mean I was officially his girlfriend? Probably not. The question is, how do I get him to ask me out again? Why was he so interested in the old Alice and not in this one? This one is so much better. I look better, I'm more popular, and I feel a whole lot happier.

I'm afraid that he's about to leave the kitchen without noticing me, so I move between him and the door and say, "Hey, Seth. How about a dance?"

Did I really just ask him for a dance? I'm definitely more confident, then. Finally he focuses on me and he looks a bit panicked. Also, he's blushing. It's meant to be me who blushes. Seth was always so self-assured when we were together. Weird.

"Sorry," he says, "I don't dance, I'm useless at it."

"So am I," I tell him, "but I don't let that stop me."

He laughs, politely. "No, really, I'd rather not, thanks."

There's an embarrassed silence. I realize that he wants to leave and I'm blocking his way. I sidestep casually and let him through, but my heart is beating fast. I can't believe it! He's just turned me down! Now what? I can hardly run after him and say, "But Seth, you like me, remember?"

Of course! It's probably because he knows I'm going out with Luke. God! I've just made a complete fool of myself. What will he think of me now? I must seem like a total flirt!

Chapter Six

Suddenly I become aware that I'm not the only person in the kitchen. It's a big, open-plan kitchen with a dining table and sofa and TV at the other end, and I realize that Chelsea and Clara have been sitting on the sofa the whole time. Great. I glance over at them, expecting to see them sniggering. Instead they wave.

"Hi there, Alice," says Chelsea.

"Don't worry about him," says Clara, "he's in a mood because he asked Lauren to the party and she wouldn't come."

"Lauren?" I say incredulously as I go over and sit with them. They seem perfectly happy to see me and not at all horrible. In fact they're up for a good gossip.

"Apparently," says Chelsea, leaning in and putting on a fake whisper, "Seth asked Lauren to the party but because Sasha didn't invite Imogen, Lauren wouldn't come and said she was going to spend the night at Imogen's to keep her company—or something like that."

"Lauren? Imogen?" I know I sound dumb, but I can't help it. What's going on?

Luckily I can count on these two to fill me in.

"Yeah," says Clara. "Sasha made a big deal about handing out the invitations and made it perfectly clear that Imogen wasn't invited, which is silly really because everyone knows she wouldn't have come, anyway. Then, when Seth asked Lauren, she turned him down because she was going to Imogen's."

Déjà vu, or what? I realize that the person standing with Imogen in the photo on my bedroom wall must have been Lauren. Obviously Lauren is now Imogen's best friend. And it sounds like she's being a better one than I was and isn't sneaking off for a date with Seth. Well, good luck to her. I hope they're having a boring time together.

Okay, so I feel momentarily jealous. I know I chose not to be her best friend. I just didn't realize that it was going to be so weird. I imagine them in Imogen's bedroom and I wonder if Imogen is showing Lauren the boarding-school website and if Lauren is as upset as I was. Probably she'll be glad for Imogen, like I should have been if I'd been a better friend. Since this party hasn't been crashed, I expect Lauren talked Imogen out of that crazy idea. Like I should have done. If Imogen does leave to go to boarding school, I'll make sure that Lauren isn't left on her own. I'm sure there's room for another one in our group.

I remember the row that Imogen and I had and all the horrid things she said to me. Suddenly they're all meaningless, because that was the old Alice, and she was right. That Alice was selfish and miserable and a cow to her mum and brother, but this one isn't like that. I'm busy mulling over all these thoughts when Sasha comes in.

"We were just talking about your stepbrother," says Chelsea, grinning at her.

I realize I'm tensed up, waiting for the cutting remark from Sasha, but instead she says, "Hi, Alice, glad you could make it."

"What, even though I'm such a 'lame' dancer," I hear myself saying, half jokingly. Sasha looks puzzled. "I heard you and Seth arguing," I explain. "Something about betting him fifty quid to get into my pants?" I can't believe I just said that! And to Sasha! No one seems to think that I'm acting out of character, though, so I'm obviously starting to behave like the Alice that they know. What's more, it feels right. I'm beginning to realize that being shy is a complete waste of time. I don't think I've blushed once all evening.

Chelsea and Clara are laughing about the pants thing.

"God, sorry," says Sasha, looking, I'm pleased to see, suitably ashamed. "Please don't take it personally. It's just that he winds me up so much and I knew it would annoy him. I can't help myself.

He's such a boring old fart. It was bad enough when Mum remarried, but now that he's come to live with us it's like having two new dads."

"I thought he fancied Lauren, anyhow," I say, a lump in my throat. I'm still smarting from the rejection.

"He probably only asked her out because he knew it would wind me up," says Sasha. "With her being Imogen's best friend and everything. He knows we don't get on."

"But if he wanted to wind you up," I say, "why didn't he just ask Imogen out?"

Now they're all laughing. I seem to have missed the joke.

"He's hardly going to ask Imogen, is he? I mean, she's way too scary. He only goes for shy girls because then he can be in control."

While it's all very nice sitting here and having a good gossip, it does strike me that while these girls aren't being horrid to me they are still being a tad bitchy. I mean, that could be me they're talking about—the old me. Did Seth only ask me out for coffee in the old life because he wanted to wind Sasha up?

"Have you thought that maybe it's because he's shy himself and doesn't feel comfortable with someone who's loud and confident?" I say.

"Shy? Seth? You mean repressed and boring," says Sasha. "I wish he'd stayed at that bloody boarding school instead of coming here and ruining my life."

I'm tempted to point out to her that if they stopped winding each other up all the time then her life needn't be so bad. But what's the point? She'll just think I'm crazy and won't take any notice. Suddenly I'm bored with all this. Why do people say their lives have been *ruined*? Ruined lives involve death and destruction, not some minor domestic inconvenience.

Lucy comes into the kitchen to get a drink. I wander over trying to look casual.

"Lucy? You know me and Luke?" I leave the question dangling, hoping she knows more than me.

"What!" she squawks, spluttering her drink all over the counter.

"You know, me . . . and Luke?"

"Don't tell me he's finally plucked up the courage to ask you out! Come on, tell me all about it!"

I'm a bit confused, so I tell her what I know, about him coming to fetch me and holding my hand in the park.

"Oh, my God. I don't believe it! Everyone knows he's fancied you for years, but you've always put him off. Don't tell me you've changed your mind."

"No . . . no, I haven't. It's just that . . . I do really like Luke—but just as a friend. Oh, God, I didn't realize. . . ."

"He told Miranda, before he left to get you, that he wanted her to arrange a game of spin the bottle later and that he wanted her to fix it so that he could get to kiss you," she says, laughing. "So, finally you two are going to get it together. Thank God!"

"No . . . I can't go out with him . . . I thought . . . Oh, never mind, it's complicated. What am I going to do?"

"You'll have to tell him," says Lucy firmly. "You can't string him along. Or . . . I know . . . go out with him for a bit, and then let him down gently. He has put you on a bit of a pedestal. Maybe if he gets to know you—as a real person—he'll realize you're not the goddess he thinks you are."

"Well, thanks!" I say.

"You know what I mean. Anyhow, it would certainly dispel some of the sexual tension that's always hanging around our group."

I consider the thought of going out with Luke. "I don't think it would be very fair to him. You know—if I was just pretending. Besides," I tell her, lowering my voice, "I fancy someone else."

"No! Who?"

"Seth," I whisper so that the girls at the other side of the kitchen can't hear me.

"I thought he'd asked Lauren out," says Lucy.

"I know," I say miserably. "But she didn't come, did she?"

"What a mess," says Lucy.

"Look, you know that game of spin the bottle? Could you fix it for me to kiss Seth?" I'm sure he'll realize I'm the girl for him if I could just get him to notice me.

"God, you have got it bad," says Lucy. "I could, but only if you sort it out with Luke first."

"Okay, I'll do it now," I tell her, sounding a lot more positive than I feel.

Chapter Seven

Back in the living room, I sidle up to Luke and tell him I want a private word with him. He looks dead pleased, and I feel really mean as I lead him into the now empty study.

"About earlier," I say awkwardly. I'm about to explain to him that I don't think our going out together is such a good idea.

"I know . . . I'm sorry about that," he says, in a rush. I know he's referring to the fact that he was about to kiss me on the merry-go-round. "I shouldn't have . . . it was stupid. I don't know what came over me, or rather I do. I've fancied you forever . . . well, you probably know that."

He's fiddling with the lamp on the desk and my heart gives a little lurch. He's so nice. "Let's pretend it never happened?" he says. I stop myself pointing out that it didn't actually happen. Obviously, in his mind at least, it did.

Miranda comes bursting in through the door.

"Come on, you two," she says, dragging us out, "we're about to start a game of spin the bottle."

Everyone's in the living room. All the girls are sitting in a big circle and the boys are scattered around the room. Even the Sixth Formers are joining in, but I can't see Seth anywhere. Then Lucy comes in, pulling him behind her.

"Look who I found hiding in the kitchen," she says, pushing him on to the sofa. I can see he doesn't look too pleased, but he stays put.

The game begins and a few couples go into the hall and return looking either embarrassed or ecstatic, depending. Ryan is chosen as the next boy up and Chelsea spins the bottle. It lands on Sasha. Well, there's a surprise. I detect a setup, and I'm not wrong.

They're out there for ages, and in the end, Chelsea has to go out and drag them back in. Then Seth is chosen and Lucy spins the bottle. I hold my breath. I don't know how she does it, but it lands on me. I grin broadly and then remember what Sasha said about him liking shy girls so I tone it down and try to look coy.

When we get out into the hall there's an embarrassed silence. I'm waiting for him to take me in his arms and kiss me, but he just stands there.

Eventually he says, "You don't mind if we just pretend that we've kissed, do you?"

This is awful. Why does he keep rejecting me?

"Are you going out with someone?" I ask him.

He shuffles his feet. "Not exactly."

"Well, neither 'exactly' am I, so there's no harm. It's only a kiss." And before he can object again I grab him by the front of his T-shirt and start kissing him. His lips are sort of stiff beneath mine. I make mine all soft but keep the pressure on, waiting for him to get into it. It's not long before I admit defeat and pull away. I feel so humiliated.

I go back into the living room, but Seth doesn't follow me. Instead he disappears up the stairs. Everyone's looking at me. "What have you done with him?" asks Ryan.

"Oh, he had to go upstairs and lie down to recover," I tell them with a forced giggle. They make noises at this and then the game resumes and I sit back down in the circle. I'm all churned up. *That* didn't happen like it was meant to. I'm mortified—and cross, I realize. Even if he didn't want to kiss me he could have made an effort. It's only polite. It's not like I've got leprosy, although that's how he made me feel. I'm not sure I like him anymore.

I decide to forget about the last ten minutes. Who needs boys, anyway? I'll be far too busy having fun with all my "new" friends. Before I know it I'm off in a daydream about all the things we'll be doing together and how much fun school will be. I don't notice that Miranda has grabbed the bottle and that it's swung toward me and that Luke is the next boy up. Lucy obviously hasn't kept her up to date and she thinks she's doing Luke a favor.

There's nothing for it but to go out into the hall with him. There are a few catcalls from some of his male friends as we leave the room.

We stand in the hall and, for a moment, I think that he's going to make an excuse not to kiss me as well. I wouldn't blame him.

"Well, Miss Watkins, I suppose we'd better get on with it," he says, sounding like Sean Connery from a Bond movie. "We wouldn't want them to have to send out a search party." He's grinning at me, and he takes my hand and pulls me toward him. "Brace yourself, I'm coming in."

The kiss starts off a bit funny because I'm laughing. But then he puts his hand very gently on the back of my head and pulls me into it. It's not that fireworks go off or anything but my insides do go all mushy. It feels wonderfully comfortable and familiar. I even venture to put my hands around his waist. My heart is beating fast and I realize that it's excitement and something else that I'm not familiar with. Love? Lust? I don't know, but I'm fairly sure that when Seth kissed me it was only pounding with nerves. Kissing someone you know you like is completely different from kissing someone you think you fancy, I decide.

Eventually they do send the search party out. The living-room door opens and Miranda comes out. "Stop it, you two," she says, "the game finished ages ago."

We go and join the others. As we start dancing, Luke says in my ear, "Do you want to pretend that *that* didn't happen?"

"We'll see," I say, and as I dance I can't stop smiling.

I don't think I'm a complete floozy. I just didn't see what was under my nose. I remember, in the old life, Luke coming into the art room and asking me to the party. I guess he's always liked me. Even the other me. If Seth isn't interested in me because I'm not so shy anymore, then that's his problem. I'm not going to pretend to be something I'm not.

We dance wildly and at one point I'm aware of Seth standing in the doorway watching. I think about going over and dragging him onto the dance floor, but somehow I can't see him enjoying it. Sasha's right. He should loosen up a bit, I think, looking at Luke who's trying to dance and balance a banana on his head at the same time.

I know I should feel strange hanging out with these people, because I've hardly ever talked to them before and now we're bosom buddies, but it doesn't feel peculiar, it feels right. Natural. As if it was meant to be.

I let the music flow through me, and I know that this is going to be a great life—because I'm going to make sure it is.